Of Passion and Ink

New Voices from Cameroon

Of Passion and Ink

New Voices from Cameroon

STORIES

Edited by Dzekashu MacViban

BAKWA

This publication is made possible, in part, thanks to support from the University of Bristol, Phoneme Media and Goethe-Institut Kamerun. We offer heartfelt thanks to these organizations.

Bakwa Books
Kazi Hub, CAMPOST Rond Point Express, Yaounde
www.bakwabooks.com

ISBN: 978-1-7337526-0-2

Artwork by Danielle Eog Makedah
Cover design by Dante Besong

CONTENTS

Introduction

"Where can we read contemporary Cameroonian writers?" More often than not, in the middle of good-natured banter, the question always finds its way into the conversation. I always answer it without hesitation, recommending a few writers as well as pointing them to *Bakwa Magazine*. Yet, the question never ceases to linger at the back of my mind, a famished figure that will not be staved off with crumbs.

Prior to this, there were the recurrent pieces, in which critics agreed to disagree, on paucity, publishing, and ghettoization. There was also Joyce Ashuntantang's interview by Dibussi Tande, where she emphasized the importance of owning our narratives, stating that: "As long as foreign publishers remain the midwives of our stories, they will keep determining the nature of these stories." The relevance of this statement cannot be overlooked when the legitimization of African literary output is usually dictated in New York, London, or Paris.

Bibi Bakare-Yusuf, co-founder and publishing director of Cassava Republic Press, brilliantly sums up the relationship between telling our stories and owning the means of production. In her keynote speech at the third Abantu Book Festival in Soweto, South Africa, she said: "It is not enough for us to say we must tell our own stories, if we don't equally think or talk about the enabling infrastructure that supports the generation of those stories, the infrastructure that enables the circulation of ideas and the flow of knowledge."

It therefore comes as no surprise that Bakwa's birth was underpinned by the quest to contribute to the emergence of an enabling infrastructure in our context. I've always been fascinated by how to leverage the opportunities offered by technological advancements to curate and publish stories across multiple platforms. This, perhaps, explains the fluidity that characterizes projects by Bakwa, from the written word online to podcasts and print.

That said, this book emerged as a sort of response to Africa39 and its brilliant stories, which highlighted the absence of Cameroon in the constantly evolving negotiation of literary spaces on the continent.

Drawing from similar projects by *Kwani?* and *Saraba*, the *Bakwa Magazine* Short Story Prize was thus created as a one-off project to celebrate emerging Cameroonian writers who were 39 and below at the time. Beyond the accomplishments of the prize, this was inherently a community-building initiative, an archival project, and an attempt at disrupting the status quo. The culmination of the initiative—this book—is therefore a combination of stories selected from across the longlist and commissions.

The Cameroonian literary landscape has changed radically in the years during which this project has been in production, necessitating continuity, albeit in a different form. Thus, the title: *Of Passion and Ink*: *New Voices from Cameroon* suggests our intent to continue showcasing new voices, across similar publications.

If the variety of the stories in this collection is an indicator to go by, the possibilities and realities explored by contemporary short stories from Cameroon are infinite and subvert what the world believes to be the Cameroonian short story. From Bakwa Magazine Short Story Prize winner Bengono Essola Edouard's title story, "Of Passion and Ink", which shuttles between hallucinatory realism and dark fantasy, through Nkiacha Atemnkeng's speculative piece, Monique Kwachou's psychological realism, to Dipita Kwa's social realism, these stories fictionalize different Cameroonian realities.

There's an almost inexhaustible list of people without whom this book would not be possible. However, we owe special thanks to: our partners, *Phoneme Media* (especially David Shook); Goethe-Institut Kamerun; short story judges Ba'bila Mutia, Donna Forbin, Edwige Dro, Jean-Claude Awono, and Madhu Krishnan; translators Hannah Jakobsen and Emma Fredgant; and copy editors Kayley Emiko Okamura and Nfor E. Njinyoh.

We hope the thrill that fuelled the development of *Of Passion and Ink*, which marks Bakwa's inroad into print publishing and the birth of Bakwa Books, translates into delight for the reader. This is to great stories to come... Cheers!

Dzekashu MacViban

January 2019

THINGS THE WORLD DIDN'T TELL YOU

Howard Meh-Buh Maximus

Every evening, your father tore a page off the Bible, steeped it in water, and chewed. Every evening, he mumbled the same two-minute prayer before eating the Word of God. He chewed gingerly, steadily, reverently. It may have dropped forewarnings before it started, this thing, but you must have missed them all. One evening, as the sun went to sleep, he brought out his stool and his shiny black Bible, sent you to bring him water in a bowl, before he started with Genesis.

He was on Kings now; Solomon's Splendour, like shreds of bush meat, being crushed between his teeth. Sometimes, as you did the dishes outside, or harvested waterleaf from the congregating sprouts, or as you placed a pot of water on the fireside, waiting for it to boil, you would watch him keenly, and in his eyes, you would see sureness—splinters of meanings you were certain you would never know.

When his ritual was done, you would wash him in the dimness of the bathroom—a bathroom with no mirrors and a broken door, as if it was proof that the world had broken in and stripped you of everything you had, as if just one dimension of the life you were living was one dimension too many—you did not need another realm to make it any clearer. In the bathroom, there would be silence, except for the splashing sounds made by the lukewarm water as it broke on the bathroom floor. You would scrub his hard, wrinkling flesh, your hands in a soaped sponge glove, and wish that one day, in scrubbing his body, you could scrub off the shadow too, this shadow that had stuck to his being like slime on a snail, slime that even alum could not get off. And then you would dab his skin dry with a brown towel and throw a loincloth around him. You would feed him bitterleaf soup and watch him fall asleep on the worn-out sofa, wondering what his dreams were.

Every morning, before your father woke up, you would be on the road to school. School was different, less depressing. Everyone carried their problems in their backpacks and their zipped purses and pretended to be fine. Unlike home, you knew the answers to the questions they asked here:

What is the formula of a straight line?

Explain Rainfall.

Conjugate the verb "Être."

And then there was Save, the boy for whom your heart somersaulted. The boy you would grow to love.

The first day he spoke to you was the day you faced the Disciplinary Council for breaking another student's head with a bottle. He had walked up to you in his neat blue jacket, clutching a hymnal, his gait holding such measured piety he looked like a clergyman. You sat alone in the dining shed before the food sellers came, staring into a book you were not really reading.

You were startled when he spoke to you. "Hey," he said and you nodded—did not hold his gaze. You were startled too when he sat down, mumbled a couple of things you would not remember before telling you that girls should not be fighting. You looked at him, wanted to ask why. Was it that girls did not have hands to fight, or did they just lack the ability to be angry enough to? You wanted to ask him: so if humans are basically animals and the only thing that really differentiates them, according to biology, is the development of the brain, the intelligence, and males are, according to statistics, more intelligent than females, does it not mean that females should in fact be the ones fighting everywhere? But you did not ask him this. Instead, you told him that boys should not sing soprano in a choir. You shut your book and said, in fact, that boys should not be into choral music at all.

Later, he would tell you that it was the way you said it that had made him ask you if you would like to hang out the next day, and you would wonder how you had said it. You had said no when he asked, though. And he had insisted on walking you home that day because, "When so many are lonely as seem to be lonely, it would be inexcusably selfish to be lonely alone."

"What?"

"Tennessee Williams."

You rolled your eyes, "Did I tell you I was lonely?"

He smiled, and it half-irked you, half-enchanted you, that he would smile like that.

When hours ago he had told you, "I am Save," you had gushed out an, "I knew it. I knew you were one of those preacher people."

And he had laughed and laughed, "I did not say 'I am safe...in God's name,' or that sort of thing. I meant my name is Save."

"Oh," you had said sheepishly, "I am Ramatou."

B

You walked past the students cramped in groups, yelling at flying taxis, past the woman who had in front of her a big bag of freshly harvested corn, and the man in the suit who was hitchhiking because his car had just broken down. When he tried to take your hand, you recoiled into yourself like your name was Mimosa Pudica. You walked past Mile 2, watching the endless green that sandwiched the road. He was telling you a story of what had happened to him in boarding school—Bishop Rogan College. How two boys had fought over a CKC girl, punching each other in the face until they were moist and gory with blood, how one had senselessly told the rector, when he asked what in God's name was happening here, that the other had snatched his girlfriend. "Can you imagine? Future priests, in a minor seminary." He laughed at his own story.

"So why did you leave BIROCOL? You don't want to be Father Save anymore?"

He laughed, "I actually still want to be. I just wanted to try out life in a Day School and Mixed School before I finally go."

You gave him a look, a playful smirk, "right."

B

At the intersection leading to your house, you asked about his parents, "They better not come to my house thinking I have kidnapped their son o." He laughed and said they'd travelled, "So even if I go home now, I'd be going to an empty, boring house."

Your father was inside when you got home. You wanted Save to stay outside while you changed out of your uniform, but he insisted on coming in. "I want to greet your parents." He was the kind of boy who would come to a girl's house and want to greet her parents before anything else. The kind of boy who was used to parents gawking over him, willing their kids to draw from his mellowness, his gentility. And so he got in and you could swear he almost bowed as he said "Hello Daddy, good afternoon." But your father just looked at him and looked away—focused on the sheets of old newspapers he was flipping. You started to hear your own heartbeat. Outside, he said, "I don't think your father likes me," and you laughed, and he said it was nice to see you laugh, even if it was at his pain, and you laughed again and said, "Pain? You can be a drama king eh."

That evening, as you sat under the mango tree talking about the Senior Prefect who thought his post was a money-making job, asking for bribes from latecomers and badly dressed students, as he talked and talked about how he had been seeing you around, how he thought you interesting and was looking for a way to say "hey", as you restrained yourself from telling him you've had a crush on him for as long as you could remember—the fine quiet boy from boarding school, you watched in horror as your father walked out of the house, carrying a stool and bowl of water, his Bible tucked under his arm. You watched him watch your father tear a page from the Bible, steep it in water, and chew. You watched the discomfort as it moved like a creeping thing from Save's body right into yours.

$\mathcal{B}$

He texted that night to say he had fun. "Me too," you replied. You thought about him, about how he was so tall and skinny he looked like a tree—a long, slender tree—about how his fairness made him look even more fragile, about how he laughed so much it made you laugh as well, how his unwavering joy seemed to envelope your sorrow and engulf it. It made you think of endocytosis. You thought about what he thought about your father, and when you woke up the next morning, you hated him for knowing. You hated yourself for letting him know. You should not have allowed him in your house, allowed him to see your father eat the Bible. And so in school you avoided him, pretended not to see when he waved at you. The principal, short and bespectacled, strapped in a too-tight jacket, stood in front of the entire school during assembly and announced your suspension, punishment for breaking another student's head.

Save came to your house after school that day but you did not let him in. He kept coming until one day, the sky was on his side, turning so thick and grey you knew it would rain its approval, so you opened the door and let him in. In your room, you told him that your father had not always been like this. You told him the story: how your father was a pastor, a big one with a big church, until three girls announced that he had molested them and his world started to crumble. You told him how your parents and you had grown as thin as broomsticks from too much thinking and too much fasting. Fasting for his congregation to see the light and realise it was all a lie. But it never happened. You told him how you stopped believing in love because you had not seen any stronger than your parents', how your mother had been by his side throughout the incident, telling everyone who cared to listen that her husband was innocent and those girls were the Devil's agents. And then one day, she had taken you out to the market and bought you so many toys you thought Christmas had been brought to June, how later that day, you and your father waited for her to join you for dinner but she did not. How you waited for her at breakfast the next day but she did not show up, how you waited and waited until you finally accepted that she was never going to show up.

You told him how for a whole week, you did not hear your father talk. How one day, he brought out his Bible and made a meal of it. You told him you have stopped believing in love.

He brought your lecture notes home to you with fancy cups of coffee, and you studied under the mango tree. You watched him pray before peeling a mango, before drinking his coffee, watched him pray before opening his book to read. He was the only person you knew who did not forget to pray after a meal. Because of him, you started to get closer to God; because of that, you started to feel lighter. Now, when you washed your father in the dim bathroom, you smiled and sang the songs he sent to you. When your father slept, you prayed that his dreams were beautiful.

The next weeks would smile on you, as if someone, on a fine morning, had brought you a gift you did not expect. An expensive gift you could not afford. It had been a while since you received any gifts. The last time was the day your mother left.

You would walk hand in hand to Down Beach and cosy ice-cream parlours, and when you were sure that your father was still asleep, you would sit with him, watching the young men in dirty, sagging shorts carry bags of cement. You would watch the structure they were building from the ground up, and you would think of it as yourself; you would think of Save as one of these boys, as all of these boys, building you up anew. It would be a boutique, this building, a boutique with shiny expensive things. It would be the boutique where, years from now, you would find a smiling mannequin that looked disturbingly like Save.

$\mathcal{B}$

A week before the GCE, you realised how hopelessly in love you were with him. It happened on the day he called you at midnight, crying, telling you that his life does not seem to belong to him. That there are things he wanted to do that he could not, and that his parents were pushing him to the wall. He felt like an animal, bound by chains, locked up in a cage.

"How do you mean?"

He sobbed, "It's fine, Rama. I'm fine."

You wanted to run to his house and let him cry on your chest so that you could caress him back to normalness. And yet you felt guilty finding solace in his instability. That he seemed broken like you made you feel like your pieces could complement each other, form something whole, something firm.

When you went to his house the next day, he seemed fine, laughing and talking at the table with his parents who asked you if you were the classmate he said helped him with his math. You smiled tightly and said yes. That was the first time you fought.

"Math tutor? Is that what I am to you? The classmate who helps you with your math?" He stuttered, "But you do help me with my math." You looked at him, eyes bulging, you walked away. He called to tell you that you were overreacting, you know how parents behave.

The next time you fought was when you went to his house for the second time. The maid had served you a glass of freshly squeezed orange juice which you sipped gently as you watched the music video of an elderly priest who basically sat there singing whilst the rest of the choir swayed. On the way to the kitchen to drop your glass, you overheard the maid tell his mother that your father was a madman, and that madness is likely to run in the family. The glass fell from your hand, and before Save came out from his room, you were gone.

"You left before I came out, why would you do that?" He asked when he called.

"Ask your mother."

"What? What has my mother got to do with this?"

Later, he called again. "She said she doesn't know what you are talking about. Rama…"

"So, I'm a liar, or a mad person who doesn't know what she is talking about?"

"What?"

You turned off the phone and avoided him for a week. Told yourself you were never going back to that house.

ℬ

But good news is the water that quenches fires angry decisions have made. Acing the GCE was the good news. Two days after the GCE results were released and you were still celebrating. You returned home from Down Beach with Save, arms wrapped around each other, to find your father hanging from the mango tree, a noose around his neck. The shock was so much you fainted in Save's arms. When you woke up, you did not tell him about the little relief you felt. About how your father had taken your hands and smiled joyously when you told him you had all five papers. How his death made you feel like he had been hanging in there, waiting for you to achieve something before he left this world that had stopped making sense to him. No, you did not tell Save any of this. But you let him comfort you, you watched him call home, telling them he would be spending the night with you since you lost your father. He walked away to complete the call. He returned and said, "I'm staying the night." That was the night you unbuttoned his shirt. The night you made love for the first time.

ℬ

A few weeks after your father's burial, you stared at his picture, reminding yourself of how much you looked nothing like him. How he always said you were a spitting image of your mother and the only thing you got from him was his brain. How your mother would laugh and say, "thank your stars for that, Rama; at least you look like a human being," and your father would quip, "at least you think like one." You stopped yourself from thinking about your mother. She did not deserve your thoughts.

ℬ

University application forms were made available and you'd wanted to go to Buea and get copies for you and Save. He had been such a rock and you truly felt safe with him. Sometimes you wondered how you could be so lucky, and it surprised you that you still thought yourself lucky after losing everything. You were lucky because you still had him.

You called him a week later and told him you were ill. He ran to your place, holding a bag of sugary pastries and two fancy cups of coffee. You asked him what illness coffee cured and he chuckled. Sitting on your bed, you wanted to tell him. It was when you cleared your throat that he said, "Ramatou, there is something we need to talk about." How did he know? You asked yourself, your heart thumping in your chest.

"I am going to the seminary."

You looked at him, waited for him to laugh. He did not.

"Everything is set and it is almost time."

"What?" You said, realising how light your 'what' sounded, how weightless. Your eyes trailed as he talked about enjoying his time with you. You watched his long slender fingers and clean fingernails; the young sprouts of beard on his face looked out of place, like grass growing on a wall. He was talking about his mother, how she had promised God that her child would serve Him if He gave her a child. How he had no choice in the matter. He had been groomed to be a priest. You felt something aching in your chest. You wanted to laugh, ask if his mother was bloody Hannah from the Bible. But you collected yourself, told him you love him. He told you he loves you too, but as it is, God needs him. "God doesn't need you," you yelled. "He is God, He is ultimate. He doesn't need you. *I* need you."

"God is my saviour," he yelled back. It surprised you because you had never heard him yell before.

"But you are mine." You said, "you saved me, Save. You cannot leave me now. Not now, Save. I love you."

"I love you too, Rama, but I love God more. Please don't make me choose." And then he paused, "you know, I really thought you'd be happy for me."

You could not believe him. "Are you serious? Happy?" He said you were being melodramatic, that he had told you his dreams when he first met you. That was when you lost it; seized your father's half-eaten Bible and shot it at him. He ducked and the Bible hit the coffee cups on the nightstand and fell on the floor, you were screaming "Get out! Get the hell out of my house."

"Ramatou?"

"Get out!"

You watched him leave, knowing you would not see him for a very long time. You hadn't even told him yet. You wouldn't. You wrapped your arms around your belly tight. You thought of finding a knife, of stabbing it so many times the baby in it would die.

ℬ

Nine years passed and you did not see Save, did not hear from him. Before he left, he called but you did not pick up the phone. The day you strode to his house to work things out, his mother smiled at you and told you he left yesterday. You felt your heart fall to your stomach. You saw him every day though, in eight-year-old Hope, in his tall ranginess, in his fair skin that glowed even in struggle. You saw him when Hope laughed, in the sharp dimples on his cheeks that pierced your heart; and sometimes you would hug him too tight, or flog him too hard because he reminded you too much of the man you loved, the man who left you.

It was two months after his ordination that you heard he was coming from Bamenda to visit his hometown and celebrate mass at the Holy Family parish in Bota. The person described him as one fine yellow Father who went to GHS Limbe. "Don't you know him? Father Matute Save. Their family house is in Sokolo."

You swallowed and decided to go there and see for yourself. He was surprised when he saw you, almost shocked. You had walked up to him after mass, Hope attached to your arm. You told him he looked different. His biceps were huge and he wore reading glasses, and facial hair defined his face now. "Do you people have gyms in that seminary?" He laughed. He still laughed a lot, it would seem. He told you you looked the same, beautiful as ever. You shrugged the compliment off and asked Hope if he was not going to greet Father.

You met later; he came over to your place. He wanted to know if Hope was his. You said yes, you had meant to tell him. He walked to the window and stood there for a while, silent. Later, he told you he felt at home in the priesthood. But he felt at home with you too. And you told him he could not eat his cake and have it. But then he kissed you, and you let him. You had expected him to be angry at the information about Hope, but he did not seem angry, he seemed fulfilled.

He started coming often, bringing fancy cups of coffee and toys for you and Hope. He would carry Hope on his shoulders and run around the compound laughing. In his shorts and T-shirt, any passer-by could tell it was his son. You would watch sometimes, lost in paradisiacal realms, imagining possibilities. The times he spent the night, you would wait for Hope to fall asleep before he snuggled next to you, and in the morning, he was out before the boy was up. He had clothes at your place; his toothbrush was there too. You felt again what you had not felt for nine years—consumed, whole.

Neighbours had started to talk such that one day, Hope walked up to you and asked if Father Save was his real father. You looked at him confused at first, and then told him Father Save was everyone's father, including yours. That was why everyone called him Father. He nodded and walked away. You knew he was not satisfied.

ℬ

One morning, a day after he spent the night, you told him, resting on his chest, playing with the strands of hair on it, that he should quit the seminary and join you and Hope so you can start afresh "as a proper family." He said that was not possible. "Everything is possible," you said.

"Not this, not this one."

"Why? Are you afraid of what people would say?"

He looked at you, shifted away unbelievingly, called you selfish.

"Are you kidding me? You are the selfish one." You snapped, "You left me with your child for nine whole years, nine years; do you know how we survived without you?"

"You did not tell me. You had a chance to tell me you were carrying my child, but you did not. How in God's name was I supposed to know?"

"You slept with a girl, made her fall in love with you; got her pregnant, and then left her. Tell me if that is not the height of wickedness."

The room was trembling with rage. He yelled at you to stop yelling.

"Why? Are you ashamed of me? Of Hope? Tell me, are you ashamed that people would know about us? Just like you were ashamed to properly introduce me to your family." He told you that you have lost your damn mind and you said "Yes, that is what everyone in your family has been saying, that I am a mad girl from a family of madness. Is that not why you left me? Me and your son?"

He stood up, pulled up his trousers and said, "You know what, Rama, go to hell."

"You would reach there before me," you yelled back, "Get out of my house."

"I know," he said. "That is all you know how to do, push me away."

He slammed the door behind him so hard the reverberations remained with you. You fell on the floor and started to cry, you cried until your head felt like stones were boiling inside.

Hope asked why Father Save wasn't coming home anymore and you told him he had to go back to his parish in Bamenda. You did not even know if it was true. You tried to call him, but it rang out.

ℬ

News of Father Save's death came one hot evening, as you sat with Hope outside, helping him to do his homework.

"That fine Father that was newly ordained had an accident on his way to Bamenda. The other priest survived but Father Save did not. Ah, this life." The woman had said.

You felt your bones liquefy.

ℬ

For weeks, you tried to conjure the relief that had come with your father's passing. But it did not come. You could not feel any sort of relief with Save's death. People kept saying "How can a fine Father just die like that? It had to be witchcraft."

For days, you just sat there. Sometimes, when Hope was in school, you would go to Down Beach, try to remember your conversations with him. And you would roam until a bike would almost knock you down, and the angry rider would yell in Pidgin "Ah-ah, life don pass you? You nodi look road?" It was on your way back one day that you stopped at the boutique and found the mannequin standing there, smiling at you. It looked disturbingly like Save.

You took it home. Paid the salesgirl who thought you were foolish for paying all that money for a mannequin.

This thing, when it started may have dropped forewarnings, but Hope missed them all. He watched you, as he did the dishes, reciting what had become your mantra, "He is back. He is back for me. He is back. He is back for me."

He watched you chop your hair off with a pair of scissors, handful after handful, sticking it to the face and the chest of the mannequin, where you remembered Save used to have hair. He watched you dress it in the clothes Father had left behind, telling him smiling, "This is your Father Save." He watched you sleep close to it every night, the mannequin, and he would sit by your bed as you fell asleep in the mannequin's arms, probably wondering what your dreams were.

OF PASSION AND INK

Bengono Essola Edouard

Translated from the French by Hannah Jakobsen

I still remember that dream... I was walking in a vast meadow that extended to the horizon when I saw the silhouette of a woman a few metres away from me. She was sitting on the grass, wrapped in a white satin sarong that also served as a veil for her face. Her perfectly outlined svelteness pushed me to approach her. As I did so, a storm broke with vigour, saddening the azure ether. She rose as though frightened and ran forward. I decided to follow her, gradually accelerating my pace. Bizarrely, my legs numbed as I advanced. Drops of rain, of a morbid coolness, began to fall, making me shiver.

When the drops touched the stranger, her body gave off fumes, as though they were falling on white-hot wood. I stopped to observe the strange phenomenon, and it took me a few seconds to realize that the slim satin was melting, transforming into ink, crimson here and violet there. My steps stopped in front of the desolation, from which a gloomy haze still emanated. The young woman had completely liquefied as a result of the incessant rain.

ℬ

I, Emmanuel, a poor Cameroonian, possessed no fortune, no talent, except my old wood brushes that had served me since art school, and my crude aptitude for painting. Painting was my life. I sold my pieces, hoping to find redemption.

My art and I wandered here and there. It, courting cubism, rococo, fauvism, futurism, expressionism, still life, nude art, vanitas... Yes, it was all in fact frivolity. I was a frivolous artist, drawn to anything that promised beauty; I was a compulsive ladies' man, courting the fragility of art.

My art and I roamed here and there. I brushes and canvases in my arms, in the frequented and forgotten parts of the city, in the hearts of young ladies longing for saccharine adventures. Frivolous... Frivolous... Frivolous.

Frivolous, until the day that dream troubled me deeply. Upon waking, I still had the impression of having lost someone dear to me, a sentiment that haunted me for weeks afterwards. I thought about it so much that I tried tirelessly to reproduce the scene in my paintings, through ink deftly applied to canvas. I painted every scene with the deepest obsession. But a real void revealed itself through them. I found neither the right shade of violet nor crimson that fit the image of the dream stuck in my head. Frivolous until that day because I henceforth spent all of my time in the Bois Sainte Anastasie, that converted recreation area in the middle of the city of Yaounde. I spent endless hours there to glean the necessary inspiration, to find the ideal colour composition. I abandoned my lesser passions in the sole pursuit of that desire to colour my fantasy.

I had spoken about it to Sartres, an old friend. We called him so because of the way he contemplated things and I never knew what his real name was. Even if he didn't think exactly like his namesake, Sartres' ideas revolved around his existentialist theory, which his peers found strange and stupid. His Sartres bore an "s" at the end, because it was said that he defied logic in his discourse. According to him, human beings only live to prepare for death, and it's in this state of dispossession that he lived in plenitude. The only meaning in life was to prepare that plenitude, and all the things that men indulged in in this world were nothing but an insult to the Creator's plan, which was for them to ultimately return to dust. Those who knew Sartres took him for a soul illuminated by folly itself. I, on the other hand, knew that he wasn't a mental case, but rather someone whose convictions were as imposing as his figure and as smooth as his head: any attempt to reason with him slid thereon and fell behind him.

It was because of his doctrine that he took care of cadavers in a well-known morgue, refusing any remuneration. His punctuality and fascinating enthusiasm had charmed his employers who entrusted him with the position. Often, he would confess to me that he sometimes pulled open the drawers holding the bodies to look at their faces.

Oasis, that was the name of the cafe-restaurant where I met the small world that populated my microcosm. There were, among others, Solène, the waitress—a young woman with a hospitable personality; Mama Lima, her authoritarian mother, who took on a maternal role with all the young women who frequented her cafe; and, of course, the infamous Sartres. It was at Oasis that I went to retire, after my interminable days with the brush, before returning to my house. My house, or rather the small room that I rented in the area, furnished with nothing but a couchette and crowded with canvases and cobwebs.

Mama Lima's restaurant did well enough for itself. It had a pleasant atmosphere in the evenings because of the warmth of the crowd, and the music that filled the air was

perfumed by the aromas exuding from the pressure cookers.
There was only one table where no one dared to sit: that
which Sartres preferred. New customers generally got a
quick gist of his personality. Still, he didn't always sit alone:
the time at which I ended my day was that at which Sartres'
began. He would come to have a meal before going to work
at the morgue. So we would meet at that table, and Solène
would come by with her small and pretty floral apron to see
what we wanted to order. Oh, how fond I was of those
moments...

One evening, I entered Oasis, thinking about how I
hadn't yet found what I was looking for. I took a seat and
started musing until Sartres arrived. He sat, looking at me.
He knew what was wrong.

"I see you haven't yet found the colours you need," he
said.

I listened without saying a word. Solène arrived to take
our orders and left just as quickly.

"You should rather reflect on the meaning of that
dream," Sartres went on. "I think it confirms my beliefs.
You see, everything is vanity."

Solène, smiling, arrived with our orders. "Bon appétit,
messieurs."

After Oasis, I went home to my little room. I tidied the
unfinished painting and, sitting on my bed, began to look
at it. I imagined the missing crimson and violet until
Morpheus stole me away. I thus forgot to do the evening's
habitual prayer.

The next day, I found myself, once again, on the lush
lawn of the Bois Sainte Anastasie. That place, with its tall

but young trees, its public benches made of concrete, the little river trickling down its centre, and its two restaurants. It was my new world and it only cost 100 francs to access. Thus, a lot of people would come there, especially at midday: vacationers, retirees, lovebirds and, sometimes, newlyweds.

As usual, I set up an ebony easel, prepared the canvas and placed it on the easel, and began to paint the scene of the slender, melting woman in satin which had caused me so much trouble.

About fifteen metres from me was a tamarind tree under which there was a public bench facing the other direction. The two companions sitting there were inseparable: I saw them every day, because I always painted in the same location. People would come and spend time under the tamarind tree. That day, among those who relaxed there, I noticed the silhouette of a woman sitting on the bench. My subconscious immediately associated her with the ink woman, probably because of the veil she wore on her head. I immediately abandoned the painting and gently approached, slowly, step by step, until I was behind her. As if in a trance, I put forward my hand to touch her. I admit that, in that moment, I thought a storm would break out and the dream repeat itself. But she turned around, catching me unawares, my hand trembling halfway between my shoulder and her head... I was in a daze... stuck with a gaping mouth. I was thrilled by the symmetry of this young woman's face. The only treasure her blue veil left uncloaked was her light, luminous face. Light like her hands, like the sparkling radiance of silver.

Realizing that my face was finding it hard to register anything other than surprise, I got a hold of myself, lowered my arm, and said:

"I'm sorry, miss, I didn't mean to disturb you."

"What can I do for you?" she asked.

The question surprised me even more. What could she do for me? Let me gaze at her? Touch her face? No, I had a much better idea:

"If you don't mind," I told her, "let me paint you."

I didn't expect a positive response from her, but she smiled.

"That would be okay," she said

This was the first time I was seeing her, and I already liked her smile, that sensual semicircle under her nose that began and ended with her cheeks.

I thus moved my things and set them in front of her under the tamarind tree. I painted her, driven by my passion for art, much more than during my early attempts at painting. I was enthusiastic about the idea of transposing beauty, describing it with colour and effect. The woe of impossible shades didn't betide me. The canvas was full of life. Yes, I loved everything that was or promised to be beautiful.

When I had finished, I offered the painting with both hands to the woman. It was sunset. The park was beginning to empty.

"Keep it," she told me.

She got up to leave.

"Please," I asked, "tell me your name."

"Morgana. My name is Morgana."

And she left.

That night, in my little room, I contemplated the painting that I had brought back home. The violet and the crimson were history. My thoughts were now all about her. Morgana, her name was Morgana. I contemplated her portrait, that beautiful face of ink, until Morpheus carried me away. I thus forgot to do the evening prayer.

The next day, I went to the park again. I didn't sit at my usual spot anymore, which was far from the tamarind tree and the bench. I set up my things at the place where I had painted that portrait of Morgana. And it was her that I was waiting for, her alone. I sat on the bench and waited with a virtuous patience. I truly believed she would come, and come she did.

She came when the sun was at the height of its curve, when people were flocking into the park, at the moment when I would normally start looking for the violet and crimson that had cruelly haunted me.

She said hello and sat close to me, smiling. She had recognized me.

"Morgana," I said to her, "your name is Morgana."

"That's right," she said, laughing. "And what's yours?"

"Emmanuel. I'm a painter."

"I noticed."

"You're very beautiful, Morgana."

"Thank you."

She responded with the same smile, as though she wasn't surprised. She must have heard it too often, apparently. I carried on:

"Would you mind if I asked you a few questions? I would like to get to know you. I've never painted a face like yours, you know."

She smiled again, and said:

"A painter… I find you just as interesting. I've never rubbed shoulders with a painter. What if I asked you questions in return?"

I couldn't have asked for better. Morgana was letting me talk with her.

I told her my story, my life, and my love for painting. Without telling her about my dream, I told her why I was there. I told her that I had been looking for two damned shades of colour, but that those woes were now over. She told me simply that she came from far away, from another place, that she wanted to enjoy the air, the greenery, nature… She was looking for the happiness she had never had, freedom. She told me that was why she sat on the bench, under the tamarind tree, and why she stayed there, contemplating the park. I asked her why she wore a veil and she replied that she wanted to be free, free to not be seen, free to come and go, and that she would come to the woods as long as she could. I got up then, stood before her, opened my arms wide, and said to her:

"So, let me paint you, every day. Grant me that privilege, pose for me and no one else. Not nude, just as you are. I find you perfect."

"I accept," she said, laughing. "I think we'll have fun."

I therefore made haste to paint her, on the canvas already set on the easel. I painted her, driven more than usual, by my passion for the art, much more than during my early attempts at painting. I was enthusiastic about the idea of transposing her beauty, describing it with colour and effect. The woe of impossible shades didn't betide me, they were a long way off. The canvas wasn't filled with life: it *was* life. Yes, I liked everything that was or promised to be beautiful, and, even more so, that which was beautiful and alive.

Day after day, I went to the park and Morgana came. She came when the sun was at the height of its curve, when people were flocking into the park, at the moment when, before she came along, I would normally start searching for violet and crimson, those two cruel tormentors who now haunted me no longer. We talked tirelessly, throwing our heads back and laughing, humming, and I painted.

She smiled constantly. She was happy. Her eyes attracted me with an increasingly powerful magnetism. What I was yet to see was her hair. I imagined it was a deep black like her eyes; long and curly. I knew that I would never know, because she wanted to be free, free to not be seen, free to come and go.

The clouds came and went regularly as well, the sun would act shy sometimes, time passed, and the portraits grew in number with the seasons, despite the bad weather. The tamarind tree remained, an unchanging witness to this happiness. I was, then, in a position to say: "Life is beautiful!"

Every evening, we, Sartres and I, met at Oasis, a welcome reprieve from the desert-like dryness of life, where I would recount my days. Sartres listened attentively, and I saw that something about him had changed. I didn't know what, so I told myself that I was probably wrong, that Morgana's presence in my life was brightening up everything around me.

My room had them everywhere, those captivating images, those faces made of ink. It had large ones hanging from the walls, strapped to the ceiling; mid-sized ones at the back of the poorly designed door; small ones on the floor, and leaning against the wall. It was overflowing with them, but they were all of one person: Morgana, her name was Morgana. I would come in, lay down, and contemplate them all. I would try to absorb everything with a gaze, until Morpheus carried me away. The evening prayer was no longer part of my rituals.

And so time passed. Morgana became essential to my life. She became the reason I would wake up in the morning. I didn't tire of drawing her, laughing and chatting with her. I didn't tire of the concrete bench and the tamarind tree, the two silent companions to our reunions. From the first to the last day of the week, we would meet there, but monotony never made the guest list. Morgana didn't tire of being happy. One doesn't tire of being happy.

Then, something happened: I fell in love with Morgana. I no longer saw her as the ideal subject for my art, nor as the loyal friend with whom I spent every day. I saw that source of immense happiness as a woman to love. I would look deep into her eyes, into that deep black. To take the weight off my mind, I decided, one day, to tell her.

That day, we were sitting on the grass, still under the tamarind tree. The fluffy clouds, blown by the trade winds, drifted above our heads. They would cast their shadows over us at times. I had finished her portrait, which was several notches higher in perfection compared to previous days. We watched the leaves of the tamarind tree respond to the caresses of the breeze.

"Have you ever been in love, Morgana?" I asked.

"Yes, I've been in love," she responded with intensity.

"Do you currently have someone in your life?"

"You're asking me if I'm in love... No."

I stayed silent for a moment, before turning my head towards her and saying:

"Morgana... I love you. Not a little, nor even a lot, but passionately."

She, in turn, turned her head towards me. The look on her face had changed, become sour, tinged with sadness. One could have said that she didn't want me to suffer from such an affliction.

"Emmanuel..." She said. "I wasn't ready for this."

"I won't let you down, Morgana. Let me love you. Open your heart to me. Learn to love me."

We stayed there, looking at each other, into each other's eyes. She locked her gaze on me as if to test my sincerity.

"Could you go three days without seeing me, Emmanuel?" She asked.

I didn't respond, because one day without her was practically inconceivable to me.

"Give me three days to think about it and give you a reply," she continued. "Three days only. If my decision is negative, we shouldn't see each other anymore. If, instead, my decision is favourable, we'll continue to see each other, and I will love you like I've never loved any man."

I decided to give her the three days she requested. Three days after which the feeling of being loved would perhaps be revived within me. I became melancholic from the moment of our agreement until she left, and even afterwards.

That evening, at Oasis, I met Sartres, who—I don't know why—was in the grip of a melancholy even greater than mine. Solène came along and sensed that something about us had changed. Not wanting to disturb us, she left and brought the dishes that we most frequently ordered. I told Sartres what had happened to me during the day, why I was sad. He listened attentively without saying anything, as usual.

Throughout those three days during which Morgana deprived me of her presence, time passed slowly, my heart in torturous distress. It seemed like the earth was ticking over, prolonging the agonies I was enduring. Fortunately, the portraits of the young lady were there. Looking at them helped me to withstand the wait. I no longer went out to paint, impatiently waiting for the day that would seal our fate, and it finally came.

On that day, I went to the park as usual, but without any painting materials, having woken without the desire to lay my hands on my brushes. I sat on the chilly bench. With religious calmness, I awaited Morgana's arrival. I knew that she would come, and come she did.

The day went by like all the others, except that I didn't paint. We talked, we laughed. She told me that she was really happy. We stretched out on the grass, and watched the clouds passing over us. Their lazy shadows slid in irregular waves, veiling the sun intermittently. We stayed that way until the evening. The Bois Sainte Anastasie emptied, and Morgana knew that the hour had come to yield me a response. We therefore sat on the bench.

We had grown much closer to each other, compared to the days preceding those three days. Time seemed to slow down, and sensing that, I looked around… It was at that moment that the breeze blew, that the crows' threnody tore through the air. The last rays of sunlight fell like a shawl unleashed from the sky, laying their coloured contrast onto the green, dry grass. Morgana's beauty shone more than ever. The tamarind tree was in a frenzy, reacting exaggeratedly to the moving air's caresses. The whole scene was one I would have liked to paint. I waited for her to respond, revelling in losing myself in her eyes. She smiled, and I thought I read on her face that she loved me.

My gaze moved to her lips, mine moving towards hers, waiting for a, "yes, I love you," to lock with them. They finally moved, those full, red lips.

"Emmanuel," she said to me. "I love you."

I was surprised and overjoyed at the same time. I felt my heart explode with joy in my chest. The pull between my lips and hers became stronger.

"I love you," she continued, "but I refuse to suffer a second time."

Everything stopped for a moment: my heart, my breath... time... Morgana stood up and began to run. She ran towards the exit. I stayed on the spot, asking myself if it was, in the end, a negative response. In truth, I was suffocating. But I needed to follow her. I got up and ran after her, trying in vain to call out to her. But I was short of air, so I let up. She got further and further away, disappearing in the horizon like an image fading away. Only when I had completely lost sight of her did I get my breath back, slowly. After catching my breath, I sped up again.

Strangely, Morgana had headed in the direction of Oasis, which was the same as that of my home. So I stopped by Mama Lima's restaurant, utterly winded. I went past the table where I would normally seat with Sartres and headed towards the counter, all the while glancing around for Morgana. Mama Lima was bringing dishes over to the counter and Solène was arranging them carefully on a tray, in groups of three, to carry them to the tables. They stopped when they saw me.

"What happened to you, son?" Mama Lima asked. "Is the devil on your heels?"

I told them I was looking for a woman who had just come in and gave them her description. Solène replied that she hadn't seen anyone who looked like that. I left immediately, leaving mother and daughter exchanging looks of surprise.

There was nowhere else to look but my room. I got myself there quickly. While approaching, I saw the door was ajar, which gave me hope. I stopped running and walked the rest of the way. Crossing the threshold, I hoped to find Morgana there. But no... I found Sartres, on his knees, holding the most recent of Morgana's portraits in his hands. I was astounded to find him there, holding a portrait of her. I couldn't make sense of it. He saw me and read the incomprehension on my face, so he didn't take long to explain. He recounted the strange story of Drawer 027...

Sartres had indeed often confessed to me that he sometimes pulled open the drawers holding the bodies to look at their faces. I had never been able to tell if it was out of obsession or perversion. So, one night, as he was going about his usual drawer-opening rounds, he stumbled upon a face whose purity was equalled by none among all of the faces he had observed until then... The face in Drawer 027... That night, he didn't carry on with his rounds. He stayed next to that face, observing it until dawn.

From then on, every time he left the morgue, he only thought about returning to that face. He was always lost in thought, even when we were at Oasis. I had noticed that something about my vespertine companion had changed, and I was right... Sartres thought ceaselessly of Drawer 027. And when, finally, he was back at the morgue, he would no longer make rounds. He would open the famous drawer and contemplate the face... until dawn...

Then, one night, as he was beginning work, he overheard two officials of the morgue discussing the removal of the body in Drawer 027, an impending event. The next day, I entered Oasis, troubled by the fact that

Morgana would be depriving me of her presence for three days. I saw Sartres burdened with an immense sadness. He, who would always listen to me, didn't say anything… until the body in Drawer 027 was removed.

ℬ

"Last night, when I got to the morgue, I opened Drawer 027… It was empty. I opened all the other drawers to see if the body had been moved, but I didn't find it. As soon as dawn broke, I came here, to you, because you were the only person in whom I could confide. But you had already left. It was then that I noticed the strange resemblance between your paintings and Drawer 027's face. There's no doubt about it, it was her, Emmanuel. It was your Morgana," Sartres said.

"What are you talking about, Sartres?"

I thought he had lost his mind, as he tried to convince me that the face in Drawer 027 was that of a woman, specifically the one portrayed in my paintings… Morgana. Before then, he had never seen any of them, neither Morgana nor my paintings.

"Don't you know, Emmanuel?" He continued. "Don't you know that some dead come back in their physical form to savour life, to continue to enjoy the same pleasures as the living? I beg you, tell me where Morgana is so I can see her one more time. Just one more time, Emmanuel. Then you can keep her for yourself."

"I lost her, Sartres," I replied. "She is gone. She ran away. I'm so sorry."

Pain welled up within my heart as I uttered the words. Sartres tried to hold back his tears. I could tell he wouldn't be able to do so for long.

"I see," he said. "Usually, revenants leave when a close relation notices them. That's because they shouldn't be where they are. Did someone close to Morgana see her?"

Was that why she wore a veil? She said she wanted to be free, free to not be seen, free to come and go. Bizarrely, she had appeared around the same time as Sartres' dead woman and had left on practically the same day as her. As it dawned on me that what Sartres was saying was true, dry tears escaped my eyes, and I answered him:

"No, Sartres. She ran away because I asked her to love me."

Sartres burst into tears. They fell and streamed down the canvas. Where this salty, colourless ink fell, fumes escaped, and the colour came off the canvas. All the other portraits behaved as though they were tied to the one in Sartres' hands by an invisible bond. The ink on their surfaces was dissolving. Soon, the canvasses were nothing but immaculate white surfaces. All of the ink on the paintings had melted. All of the colours had fused, forming a new ink, violet here and crimson there. Just the two shades I needed to finish the paintings of the melting ink woman. Seeing the strange event unfold, Sartres stopped crying. He realized that he was experiencing the climax of my dream. As for me, I could now grasp the meaning of my dream in its entirety. Morgana was not only dead, she was also the slender woman in satin. The rumbling in the sky that had set her running was the love that I felt for her. The rain that had dissolved her symbolized Sartres' tears of sadness. I had come back to square one, but now I had the key to the problem: I had the shades of colour I was looking for; I now knew the meaning of that dream. I could finish the paintings of the slender, satin-draped woman. But was that better than her presence?

Morgana, her name was Morgana. She had surely suffered from love, to the point of death. She had come back to savour life as she never had before. And she had fled, unwilling to suffer again, to subject another to the same suffering, or rather two others. I would go to the park, but she would come no longer. Not when the sun was at the height of its curve, when people were flocking into the park, nor at any other moment. She had gone to seek plenitude in other places, far from the gaze of those who could recognize her.

Our people still tell stories of the dead who come back in their physical form. We sing the words of a wise man, lyrics that say that the dead are not dead, that we can catch hold of their voices by listening to the bush sob.

EMPLOYEE OF THE MONTH

Dzekashu MacViban

Stargazing from the top of the KICC in Nairobi was all it took for me to forget what a failure I was. Fortunately, it hadn't taken long for me to find a job at a Kentucky Fried Chicken at Kimathi Street, and my shift ended just in time for me to explore the bowels of my new hometown in the friendly dark. I embraced all it had to offer, from its decadence and exclusive soirées, to its red-light districts.

Work at the KFC was demanding, and it was usually punctuated by the omnipresence of Joroge Douglas. He was an employee who'd worked his way to a high rank—and salary—at that KFC and kept feeding me with useless crap about how I was not very enthusiastic about my job.

"At this rate you'll never be the employee of the month," he said, pointing at a picture of another new guy who'd been chosen because of his hard work and enthusiasm. There was a special section on the wall on which the placard was affixed. It was a brown placard, and on it were two square spaces for two pictures which stood side by side and were coloured yellow and white respectively. Above the yellow pictureless space on the left was written Employee of the Year, and beside it, below the inscription Employee of the Month on the right, was a picture of the douchebag who currently held the "envied" position, plus, he always smiled. "It is good for your CV, you know. Imagine how employee of the month at a Nairobi KFC could change your life," Joroge continued.

I was silent. He paused, and said, "Your hair is always unkempt. If you want to keep an afro, for Christ's sake, make it neat. You're scaring the shit out of some of our customers, and maybe you even remind some of them of the close encounters they've had with Nairobbery. Look, I'm on your side here, and I am accountable for all the workers in this KFC. If by the end of the year, your profile shows that you've never been an employee of the month or year, you can kiss your job goodbye." This guy was talking about KFCs as if his father was a shareholder and for all I knew, the motherfucker was almost as broke as I was.

One day, some of the workers at the KFC and I were making fun of Mugo, an employee who worshipped the employee of the month position, when a woman who looked like a lost angel walked in. Silence descended upon us like an ambush. She was one of those Kenyan-Indians who'd picked up the best of both worlds, and most Nairobians would kill-or-get-killed for her. Her thick, soft black hair flowed behind her like a river and her skin had the colour of chocolate. Her nails were painted black and they reflected the light-brown hazel colour of her dreamy eyes. She ordered a chicken cheeseburger and while she waited she went to the jukebox and played "Sunny" by Boney M. The mysterious girl left after a while and everybody seemed bemused as if they were in a dream from which they couldn't wake.

A few weeks later, a workshop I attended near Kifaru Garden introduced me to the wonders of photography. I didn't hesitate to purchase a Canon camera with my savings which accompanied me everywhere. One evening, a friend invited me to a hangout on 28 Kijabe Street, saying it'll be fun.

The World's Loudest Library at 28 Kijabe Street was a unique experience. A private residence made available for art. The music was soothingly serene, unlike the cacophony I'd grown up with. It was a dimly lit place which could be taken for any ordinary spot in Nairobi until the poetry performances and the spoken word improvizations started. The double-dozen people who were there indulged in smoking and drinking, and a thick cloud of smoke hung above the motley crowd, slowly spiralling under the influence of a light breeze. Simultaneously, the flickering illumination from a nearby flat, which reflected on the slowly spiralling cloud of smoke, made it look like the portal to another dimension. I stood transfixed at the door for I do not know how much time and the first picture I took was that of the spiralling smoke that looked like a breach in the space-time continuum. Later, I took a picture of the DJ. I noticed the nymph who'd purged the air of pestilence at the KFC some weeks earlier and made my way towards her.

"Hi," I greeted, as I sat down.

"Hi," she replied with a generous smile.

"I saw you at the KFC in Kimathi Street last week," I said. "You ordered, and played Boney M on the juke box."

"How come I didn't notice you? I'm pretty good with faces."

"I work there."

"Oh."

"You must think I have a shitty musical taste—my friends always tell me that—let's face it, who listens to Boney M nowadays?"

"I do. My taste is very eclectic."

"Really? No kidding, you like Boney M?"

"Yep, *Take the Heat Off Me* is my favourite Boney M album. Too bad Bobby Farrell died in 2010."

"I have an idea," she said. "Do you have an iPod with you? We can swap iPods for the hours that we'll be here."

"Cool, great idea."

We swapped iPods while those around us were swapping books. Part of the concept of the hangout included bringing books one liked and swapping them.

"So, what's your name?" I asked.

"Ciru, but my Indian friends call me Kalinda."

"I prefer Ciru."

"OK."

At length, I gradually grew unaware of the people who were around us and it seemed as if we were all by ourselves. My gaze lingered on her full luscious lips while she lit a cigarette. She took a few drags and passed the cigarette to me, assuming that I was a smoker. I wasn't into cigarettes, but I had a few drags nonetheless because I didn't want to be a killjoy. As we exchanged cigarette after cigarette, our fingers lingered for contact and our drags and exchanges became lust-laced.

A few hours later, she told me that she was going to the loo and that I should wait for five minutes and join her there. One minute later, I joined her in the loo and before either one of us could say anything, I was peeling off the dress she wore while her nails tore into my flesh and she fumbled her way to my fly. The door behind us was full of graffiti and the one at the centre, written in green on the white door said: REFUSE TO EMBRACE YOUR

MADNESS AT YOUR OWN PERIL. Everything around us faded as I entered her.

ℬ

It seemed as if Ciru had put in just the right amount of affection to revamp my existence which, at that particular point of my life, seemed to be going nowhere. I became more devoted to work at the KFC, and I still couldn't come to terms with the fact that in the past five months, I'd been made employee of the month two times in a row; much to the vexation of Mugo, the previous employee of the month. All this didn't really matter, although the bonus check did help. What really mattered was that I looked forward to seeing Ciru at the end of my daily shifts, which was at about 6:30 pm. She'd be leaning on a wall outside the KFC, listening to Liquideep on her earphones and sending me a BBM if I wasn't out by 7 pm.

We'd been to the movies at Village Market a couple of times and watched all that the box office had to offer. One night after watching a movie we decided to go for a walk. No more movies, no matatus, no Uber rides, no hitchhiking, nothing. Just the two of us walking arm in arm. We'd swapped iPods and phones so much such that we knew each other's taste well enough, so we started swapping books. Recently, she'd given me her copy of *The Thing Around Your Neck* by Chimamanda Ngozi Adichie, and I'd given her my copy of Roberto Bolaño's *The Savage Detectives*. That evening, as we were talking about writers, I told her that I identified a lot with Doreen Baingana from Uganda, because she'd lived in the US for sixteen years and in Kenya for two years, had a love-hate relationship with both countries, and wished she were Nigerian. Seeing how serious I was, Ciru understood that I was saying something that I'd kept to myself for a while and pressed me to tell her more. I told her that I'd spent a good part of my life in Cameroon, four years in the US, had a love-hate relationship with both countries, and I wished I were Kenyan. There was a brief moment of silence during which I paid attention to cars that were honking on the road. A Johnnie Walker advert stood out on a skyscraper somewhere behind us.

"I hardly talk to my parents," Ciru said after a while. "We fell out because I decided to do journalism while my father wanted me to do business because he wanted me to inherit his company. The last time I spoke to him was five years ago and he told me that I had disappointed him, that I was a crash-and-burn failure and that I'd let down the family's name. The only person I speak to on the phone now is my mother."

"Where are your parents?" I asked, noticing that she wanted to unburden her soul.

"They are in Bangalore. My father came to Kenya in the mid-seventies, fleeing the Emergency when Indira Gandhi suspended the Indian constitution. He started a new life here and got married. After about three decades, they went back a few years ago. I've been thinking about going to see them in India for a while now, but I don't know how I will face my father."

There was an awkward silence and the only noise was that of our footsteps. I said:

"My family in Cameroon thinks I'm still in the US. I was studying for a degree in ICT, but the truth is that it didn't work out well, and after a few years my visa expired and I went underground. The last time I called home, I told them that my visa had expired and I was trying to survive without one."

We reached her apartment at Riverside at about midnight. After a joint shower, I had a closer look at the shelf in the parlour which always had a magnetic effect on me while she made tea: we were both tea people. The shelf was full of phonograph records, the first three being records by Cerrone, Musical Youth, and Donna Summer. She'd once told me that most of them were gifts from her former boyfriend who was a DJ. He'd initiated her into the wonderful world of the vinyl by teaching her how to care for, appreciate and spin them, as well as play them backwards. He'd even told her that she had the potential to become a DJ, and started teaching her backstage during events as he toured in various circles in Nairobi from dusk to dawn. We talked right up to the small hours of the morning while the sound system repeated Michael Jackson's "Baby Be Mine."

ℬ

After a few days had passed and Ciru hadn't called by the KFC, I became worried. My angst worsened when she didn't reply my phone calls, so I decided to go to her apartment. It was Sunday evening and the sky behind me was red like never before, as if it were wounded. As I used the spare key she'd given me to open the door, I felt goose bumps all over my skin. Once inside, I found her sobbing in the bathtub. The dress she wore was soaked and I couldn't make out if it was due to the fact that the tub was wet or because of her tears. I rushed towards her and pulled her out of the tub, fearing the worst. She didn't seem herself and kept saying *baba, I'm sorry* between sobs. I pulled a nearby towel and dried her, holding her in my arms until she stopped crying. I made her a cup of tea an hour later before I asked her what the matter was.

"My father is dead," she said and went silent.

I was silent too for a while, and then I asked, "How? What happened?"

"I dunno," she said, and added, "I'm going to India tomorrow."

We were both silent. By now she'd stopped sobbing.

Ciru went to India the next day and that was the last time I saw her or heard from her. She never returned my calls.

CABONGO

Wise Nzikie Ngasa

"Cabongo," Mama calls and knocks at the wooden door.

No response.

She puts an ear against the door, listens and hears something: the barely perceptible sobs of a man. "Cabongo, can I come in?" Mama's voice quivers as she knocks even harder. This time, the knock is answered by a wild scream from inside. Alarmed, Mama forces the doorknob, pushes it open and runs into the room.

Cabongo shoves a woollen blanket away and jumps to the floor from a small iron bed. He is a diminutive fellow with an overwhelming head, a head that looks even bigger because of its thick mass of dreadlocks. A thin curly stream of spittle dribbles down the side of his mouth. His moustache is wild, his dreadlocks long and dirty. His eyes are white; the iris and pupils have all but disappeared. Sweat is dripping down his coal-dark face and chest. He is not wearing any clothes.

He blinks and swings his head in a circular manner. He runs his hands over his face, then his chest, and quickly down his thighs, scratching himself vigorously.

Mama stops a few metres from him. She puts out both hands and motions to Cabongo to keep calm.

"Ca, I'm here now. I can help you. What happened?" she begs.

"Ma... Ma... Mama," Cabongo stammers. "Ma, they, they cut me," he says, grabbing his neck with both hands as if he wants to strangle himself.

"They...they...they cut me and spilled my blood," he cries, collapsing down on his knees, still clutching his neck.

"I'm sorry, Babe," Mama purrs and takes a step towards him, watching his every move. "Babe, keep still and let me help you. We will fight this together. Okay?" She takes another step forward.

Cabongo begins to blink ceaselessly.

Mama has approached and is now close enough to touch him. She places her hands on his cheeks and caresses his beard.

"Babe, I'm here for you, okay?" Mama whispers. Cabongo nods.

Mama takes his hands and draws them away from his neck. She goes down on her knees and takes him in her arms. She pats him on the back, just like one would do to urge a baby to stop crying.

"Let us sit down, Babe," she pleads, pointing at the bed. She rises, pulling him up with her. They sit down on the bed, his murky dreadlocks falling all around them. Mama reaches for a band hanging on a rusted nail in the wall and ties his hair into a knot.

Cabongo is shivering like one suffering from a high fever. His feet are twitching, his eyes are rolling from left to right, his chest is rising and falling as he breathes and swallows. The room, which contains only a bed, table, chair and wardrobe, is about two square metres. The ceiling and walls are painted in black. An unwashed plate, still wet with the blood of some animal lies on top of the table alongside a bottle of salt, a stem of the Peace Plant in a clay pot and a box of incense.

"Baby, what happened? Please talk to me," Mama says.

Cabongo wipes tears from his eyes.

"Mama, they were four of them," he swallows hard. His voice is low. Mama moves closer and puts a hand across his shoulders.

"They came in through the window," he points at the small space in the wall above Mama's head, through which a stream of light flows into the room. He is rubbing his palms together, as if it helps to relieve him of some kind of pain.

"They placed me in a large eggshell and we ascended into the heavens. We swarm through beams of flashing light as big as rivers; we fought with wild claps of thunder and a wind that bites like teeth. The rain was pouring in mad torrents; the skies were mourning the end of humanity," he sobs and wipes the snot from his nostrils with the back of his hand.

"Then we came over a place of a million hills and valleys and descended from the firmaments in an illuminated mighty cloud of smoke through the open roof of an icy cave." Cabongo stops talking for a while. The air is heavy with the odour of incense and sweat. Mama stands up and opens the window before dropping down by his side again.

"Creatures were seated at a table made of bones and human skin on which were placed an assortment of knives, a bowl of pebbles and the slice of a man's tongue. Buried deep in their skulls, on each side of their heads, were two molten eyes that burned like crying torches. They were all heavily bearded, with clean-shaved heads, long-beaked mouths and sunken jaws."

Mama's eyes are wet, but she is not crying.

"The four creatures who took me to the cave went to their seats. The crumpled remains of a man's arm was making the rounds. Each of them bit a piece and passed it on."

Cabongo spits on the bare floor. His spittle is mixed with blood.

"The being at the head of the table rose from her seat, grabbed a knife and smiled at me, exposing teeth of rusted needles. She danced and waved the knife and all the creatures rose to their feet."

Cabongo makes to stand, but Mama holds him down.

"They began to chant incantations. Three creatures came forward and picked me up from the eggshell. They placed me, face down on the table. It smelled of blood and rotting human flesh. I screamed; I screamed and fought back using my nails, teeth, legs and arms. But it was of no use, Mama."

Cabongo is crying again. Mama takes his hand and caresses it.

"Finally, the creature raised the knife into the skies, shouting out my name. She brought it down with all the force in her body. My head and body went their separate ways, wallowed in the sea of blood all around me. The creatures scrambled for knives; they gathered around the table. They cut me up, ate my flesh and drank my blood. Look at my neck Ma," he cries.

Mama takes a close look at his neck. Many thin cuts run in a web-like formation around his neck. He is bleeding.

"I'm sorry, Babe," Mama says inviting him for a hug. He collapses into her arms and they remain locked in embrace until the red wetness from his neck begins to soak into her blouse. Cabongo is holding onto her so tight that she cannot free herself.

"Baby, look at me. Everything is going to be fine, okay?" Mama's voice is gentle. Cabongo nods and holds her tight. She tries to free herself from his grip, to look into his eyes, but Cabongo does not let go. His head is buried deep in the space between her breasts.

"Look at me, Ca!" she orders.

"Mama, I can't," he shakes his head, squeezes his eyes shut. "I can't, Mama, they are coming again. Please hold me, Mama!" he screams.

Mama embraces him even tighter, but his body is rocked by a wave of quakes so strong that Cabongo falls over on the bed. He punches, twitches, kicks, spits, bites. Mama falls on him, and summoning all the strength in her body, presses him down on the bed and keeps him still.

"Ma, will you leave me too?" Cabongo asks after the quakes pass away.

"Baby, I will never *leave you*. Okay? Never," Mama whispers.

"I love you, Ma," he says, looking up into her eyes. For a while Mama is unable to find the words to reply. *I love you* never felt so painful. It never felt so sweet and yet distressing to hear.

"I love you more, Baby," she sighs, tears gathering in her eyes. And for the first time in years, she lets them flow freely down her face. Cabongo reaches out and wipes them away.

ℬ

Thin, tall and white-haired, with rings of dark skin around sombre eyes, Mama can easily be mistakenly for another weary octogenarian. But she turned 54 only last week. As she lies there, running her hands through Cabongo's dreadlocks, memories of all she has had to endure over the years invade her mind.

This has been her life: fighting with Cabongo and things she can neither see nor understand; changing his diapers whenever he suffers from occasional bouts of urinary incontinence; fasting, praying... trying not to give up. At 30, when his mates are married with children of their own, Cabongo still lives in her backyard.

In many ways, Cabongo seemed normal when he was born. He cried when he came out, weighing slightly over three kilos, suckled from her breasts and slept peacefully for long hours. He was sharp and active and started walking around on his own even before eight months.

It was not until his first birthday that the manifestations began. Cabongo had fallen asleep shortly after 7 pm and Mama had put him to bed. She had rejoined the boy's father who was watching TV in the living room. And when they returned to the bedroom later to sleep, Cabongo was nowhere to be found.

They searched everywhere in the house but could not find him. They went to the neighbours and raised an alarm. A search party was soon formed. They ransacked the house and neighbourhood. They went to the police and reported the disappearance and returned home disoriented. In the small hours of morning, the couple heard the shrill laughter of a baby coming from under a bed.

They raced into the room and pulled out the mattress. Cabongo was lying underneath. He was laughing, a lurid, piercing, unsettling laughter that Mama has never forgotten.

They brought him out. His hands were tied together behind his back with a small red string, his lips red with some liquid. But there was no wound in the child's mouth or elsewhere. He seemed more excited than ever and bit his mother's finger when she tried to clean off the liquid.

Two days later, still worn out from shock and insomnia, mother and father took the child to church for special deliverance. The man of God, Prophet Boma Job was kneeling alone at the altar in the place of worship when they arrived.

As soon as they walked in through the door, he began to sing and pray. He had a Bible in one hand and a staff that ended in a cross, in the other. He asked them to kneel with him, to confess their sins, to pray against the spirits of death. He prayed in English and then in a strange language. At the heart of it all, he placed a hand on Cabongo's forehead.

"Come out!" he shouted. "Spirits of abduction, come out of this boy in the name of Jesus!"

"Amen," Mama and Papa chorused.

"Spirits of bloodsucking devils, I say come out!" he shouted pushing the child's head. Cabongo giggled and clutched at the Prophet's big thumb playfully.

When the Prophet finished praying, he gave them stickers of Jesus and holy water. He instructed them to fast for seven days. The stickers were to be pasted above every door in the house. The holy water was to be sprinkled on Cabongo's head every night before they went to sleep for 27 days. There were Psalms to read every night, unclean foods they had to desist from eating, thoughts they had to erase from their minds.

Yet Cabongo disappeared once more around his second birthday. This time, he was found in the morning, sleeping in a trash can in the backyard. Again, his hands were tied together behind his back with a red string. There were thin cuts running all over his neck in a web-like pattern and blood spilling from his mouth. Cabongo was taken to one prophet after the other and to any and every witch doctor they could afford. But the incidents never stopped.

In school, Cabongo was a truant who seized every opportunity that presented itself to stay away from class. He never took notes or completed his assignments. Yet each time he was called upon to answer a question, he always had the right answers. He never failed an exam and was always top of his class. His mates and teachers could never afford to have a misunderstanding with him. Cabongo would come to them in their dreams, they would see him in their food, in their mates' eyes, in places that would drive them mad with fright.

At home Cabongo spent his time playing video games and reading horror novels. He kept no friends. It was known, although no one ever talked about it, that Cabongo was no ordinary being.

When Cabongo turned 20, his father fled from home, leaving behind a note filled with horrific details of how Cabongo had made his life unbearable. In one part he described how Cabongo, holding a knife to his throat, had forced him to drink from a bowl of bloody water filled with the eyes of owls. In another, Cabongo flew him to the church graveyard and forced him to make love to the rotten corpse of a horse.

I am sorry, babe, he wrote to his wife. *I love you, and I once loved our son, but I can't bear this no more. I am sorry for leaving, but what was I supposed to do?*

ℬ

When Cabongo falls asleep, Mama sneaks out of his room into the main house. She takes off her clothes and goes to the bathroom.

She once believed that Cabongo would be delivered of his ailments. But after thirty years of fighting for her son, the last rays of hope she had worked so hard to preserve are all but lost. These days, food tastes like bile. Time goes by in slow motion, like a nightmare. And while she has grown weary of trying to understand the enigma that is Cabongo, her desire to give her son relief has only increased.

She turns on the shower, picks up a sponge from a soap dish and stands there staring at the falling water. As she puts out her hand to wet the sponge, the bathroom door is pushed open.

Cabongo clumps in with eyes still red from sleep. He is not wearing any clothes.

Mama turns around, startled. The sponge in her hand feels rough. There is a cold wetness below her knees from the splashing water.

"Mama, turn off the shower," Cabongo orders. Mama does as she is told.

Cabongo walks to her and takes her hands. He rubs them gently.

"Mama, I don't want this life anymore," he says and nods repeatedly as if to emphasize his point.

"Bay, you have to…"

"No, Ma, don't say a word," he whispers, cutting her off. "Just listen. I don't want it anymore, okay? No more dreams, Ma; no more madness," his voice is rising. "No more nightmares. No more pain and rejection!" Cabongo's eyes are burning with calm conviction.

"That is all, Ma. That is all," he is whispering again.

He pulls his mother's right hand towards his face and plants a long kiss on it.

"Now, go ahead and bathe, Ma," he says and stumbles out.

B

In the backyard, in a small room painted in black, Cabongo sits on his bed, drinking from a bowl. Mama stands outside the half-open door, watching him drink and whistle his favourite song. She stands there watching his every move, knowing that she may never have the chance to see Cabongo eating and whistling again.

"Ma, please come in. I know you are there," Cabongo says without looking away from his bowl.

Mama trudges in, feeling the weight of the world on her shoulders. She is carrying a bag around her neck which contains only a napkin and scalpel, but it feels heavy.

She stands in front of his bed. "Did you like it?"

"I enjoyed it Ma," Cabongo answers, licking the bowl clean with his tongue. Little drops of soup run down the sides of his mouth. "Ma, please come and sit with me," he pleads.

Mama drops by his side. When he is done licking the bowl, she takes it from him and places it on the floor. She reaches in her bag and brings out the napkin which she uses to clean his mouth.

"Ma, don't worry, everything will be fine, okay?" Cabongo beams.

"I know, Ca," Mama says. She is unable to look him in the eyes.

Cabongo is dressed in a black suit and bow tie, immaculate white shirt and black well-polished shoes. For the first time in a long while, he has shaved his hair.

"Ma, it is time," he smiles, his eyes full of glee.

"Yes, yes," she says. There is a tear in a corner of her eye.

Only a few years back, she would have done anything to see that broad beautiful smile playing on the sides of his lips. Today it breaks her heart to see him smile. "Let us say a prayer, Babe," she says.

Cabongo sits up and does the sign of the cross. He puts his hands together in front of his face and closes his eyes. Mama places a hand on his forehead.

"Help me, Lord! Help me do that which must be done! Help this soul find peace! Help him find bliss in death! May the spirit in this body know misery no more!

"Lord, I pray that 'thou-shalt-not-kill' can see and know justice. As I kill for justice, justice may I find. I pray that courage will be my portion. I pray against anguish, pain and loss. I pray in the name of Jesus!"

"Amen!" Cabongo thunders.

Mama kneels by the bed and hugs him.

"I love you, Bay," she says, her eyes red and wet.

"I love you more, Ma."

ℬ

Mama rises and steps away from the bed. Cabongo lies down on the bed, face up, staring at the ceiling. He pushes his head back on the pillow so that his Adam's apple protrudes out. He closes his eyes.

Mama is transfixed for a while. Then suddenly, without hesitation, she reaches for the scalpel in her bag. She removes it, lifts it as high as she can and brings it down on his neck, fast and hard.

ℬ

At midnight, Mama hears voices calling. She sits up from bed and takes off her clothes. She walks towards the main door of the building, in the direction of the voices. They

urge her to make haste. She quickens her steps as she goes
out of the house. She walks down the road into the dark
streets, as naked as the day she was born.

LIFESAVERS

Monique Kwachou

Fifteen-year-old Belinda made up her mind to take her life while in the bathroom on Saturday afternoon. She was bathing at 2 pm, because that's what one did during school vacations when they had nothing to do. Somehow, even if you were the kind of person who bathed routinely first thing in the morning, the fact that your brain knew you would be home all day made your body lag at going to carry water and take a bath in the dry Harmattan cold that was Bamenda in December.

She was brushing her teeth and looking around the bathroom of the family house at Ntarikon; its old tiles, and the bathtub with peeling enamel spoke of the family's middle-class history. Her granddad, Pa Achu, and his wife were, in their time, amongst the crème de la crème in Bamenda, with Pa working in the army and Mami a nurse at Bamenda District Hospital. All their children, the twins and their only daughter, went to the most prestigious schools at the time, travelling from Bamenda to Sasse in Buea, or Saker in Limbe. Belinda knew of her family's golden days courtesy of too many repetitions from Pa Achu himself, who often reminisced while chewing bitter-cola on the veranda as if to ignore the reality that he had outlived all his children. Belinda's own mother was the last to go just three months ago.

As she brushed her teeth, Belinda contemplated bathing with Ameh's Dudu Osun soap because her own Dove moisturising bar was finished. Most of her American products were finished or finishing. She knew Mami kept some stuff from the last container locked in boxes in her room, but this did nothing to make Belinda feel better. The fact that her things were finishing only added to her melancholy and reminded her just how pitiful her life had become.

As she reached out for the soap that Ameh had recently bought for herself with the intention of lightening her complexion, Belinda's eyes landed on a bottle of Advil behind the assortment of toothbrushes, squeezed-out tooth-paste tubes, and packets of sanitary pads, all competing for space on the bathroom shelf. She took out the familiar bottle. It looked like one of those her mum would have bought at CVS to send to Cameroon just a year before. How many times had she watched her mum and dad buy stuff from yard sales, CVS, Payless, Costco, and other odd outlets, packaged them and sent via barrels in a container, or in boxes through friends or distant relatives, to Mami and Pa in Cameroon or one of the numerous distant cousins and aunts? The nudge of familiarity made her turn the bottle in her hand to see the black printed expiration date, which showed six months ago. That's when she made up her mind. She would drink the bottle of expired tablets and die peacefully in sleep. It seemed like an easy way to go. No pain, just easy sleep and then when she crossed over, she would ask God what she had ever done to deserve the mess her life had become.

With her mind made up, she bathed meticulously. Her last bath had to be long and luxurious; she wanted to be found as lovely in death as Sleeping Beauty. She then put on her best house dress, the cute jersey Junior's mother had bought for her as a gift before she came to Cameroon. She thought of Junior, her half-brother, who'd probably be the only one to truly mourn her, and whom she would miss. She was the only one who accepted him as he was and did not pretend that he was not different, being autistic. She had never understood why different meant "less than" to some people, so they avoided accepting it all together.

After she'd bathed and dressed, she took the bottle of pills in one hand and the bottle of water that was always kept under the ironing table to fill the steam iron in the other. She sat on the bed, hearing the weak springs creak and screech with her movement, and shut her eyes to think her last thoughts. As though to reassure herself that she had a good reason to go against all the guidance counselling she had got on suicide in elementary and middle school back in Maryland, her last thoughts played in her mind's eye. The events of the last few months and how she had changed from the girl who had friends, her own room, and a family she could call her own, to the girl who had nothing but what boarding school lingua termed "fair-weather" friends who smiled with you when your trunk was full and had nothing to do with you otherwise.

It all began with her father's announcement that he would return to Cameroon. Her mother was confused, not because it was odd to want to go back home, but because no one had died. It also wasn't the end-of-year period fondly called "bushfaller season" for the Diasporans who returned home for the holidays. It was mid-April.

"People don't just travel back home like that!" Belinda recalled her mum had spat at her father, demanding an explanation. When her father's tale of a temporary visit to rest didn't convince her, Belinda remembered overhearing calls made to Cameroon, and her mother questioning either his siblings or friends as to why he was really travelling. Neither Auntie Louisa, Auntie Glory, nor dad's closest friend, Uncle Takor, could give a valid explanation to his sudden desire to travel home. In retrospect, Belinda understood that that period of suspicious looks and tension, built by one-word answers or no answer at all, was the silence before the storm. Because immediately after her father finally travelled, the winds that blew across the Atlantic in his wake tumbled the home and life she had known. Barely two weeks after Dad had been in Cameroon, mum received a call from Auntie Mindi. They had been watching the latest episode of America's Next Top Model and Belinda could tell it was a long-distance call as she handed the phone to her mum. The Caller ID showed "Unknown," but it was always known what country the call was coming from, if not the caller.

Belinda heard screaming and her mum got up and left the living room. Standing underneath the arched doorway leading into the dining room, she kept saying, "What? What?" Then she reverted to pidgin "Na wetin you di talk Mindi? I no di understand you, why you di hala me?" Then just as abruptly as the confusing call started, it stopped, because as Belinda turned to look at mum, she stood frozen, staring at the phone as if she could see through it, through cords across the Atlantic and into the eyes of Auntie Mindi, who had just called. Mum did not come back to finish watching the show. She didn't even ask which of the models won.

Knowing it was best to avoid breaking any rules when her mother was already angry, Belinda turned off the TV as soon as the show finished and went to say good-night early enough for her bedtime. The door of her parents' room was shut, but she knocked briefly and let herself in. Her mum looked up, holding the phone to her ear with one hand and a calling card held in the other. Her face was a mixture of impatience, anger, hurt, and confusion. Belinda said good-night, half-hoping she would be called in and told what was wrong, and half-hoping she wouldn't. All she got was a wave; theirs wasn't that kind of relationship anyway. Unlike the mums in the American sitcoms they watched, her mother did not try to be her best friend. Her mother was her mother.

As Belinda returned to her room, she thought to herself that if the walls could talk, they would tell her what the matter was, what news had ruined the evening. But then if walls could talk, hers would likewise tell of the pills she had been drinking to lose weight, hidden behind her bedside cupboard, of the times she danced naked in front of the mirror, trying to imitate the video girls, and the way she prayed fervently on her knees with hands raised to be admitted into the cool girls clique at school before Junior prom.

She fell asleep pondering on the mixed blessing that would be talking walls.

B

Belinda took the tablets one by one then two by two, filling her mouth with water after every swallow, and repeated it till she had taken 15 of the oval, reddish-brown ibuprofen, symbolic of her age. She lay down on the bed after writing a note saying she was sorry but she "couldn't take it anymore." It sounded off to her, but it was what she had seen in every movie where people took their lives. The brief perfunctory note would give the police evidence that she could not have been killed but had opted out.

She would have turned 16 in July...

She had dreamt about her sweet sixteen, prom, and everything else that would come with it once she became a teenager. She had imagined chipping in with friends to rent a limo, a white limo, to make a grand entrance to prom. She had fantasised about how she would finally be asked out by Ty Munyoki, the part-Chinese part-Kenyan head of the debate club, whom she had had a crush on ever since his presentation on Cultural Day in fourth grade during Ms Keys' class. She had imagined giving herself to him on prom night, like most girls did. She had imagined taking drivers ed, getting her first real job and saving up to help her parents buy a car.

She had never envisioned that by sixteen she would be dead by her own hand. But then nobody daydreams nightmares. Daydreams are happy hallucinations. She could not have imagined that at sixteen she'd be here with one parent dead and the other dying. She could not imagine that she would be in a school where proms were unheard of, or that she would look so ugly with her hair chopped off that Ty (had he been in this godforsaken place) would never even have spared a look in her direction.

She lay on the bed, covered herself with the bedspread, pulled it up and tucked it in her armpits like Sleeping Beauty in the illustrated Disney books. Seeking sleep and waiting for the deadly effects of the pills she had swallowed, Belinda thought of how quickly things had changed after the night of that call.

ℬ

She had gone to school the morning after thinking nothing of the fact that her mum had already left home without seeing her. Mum worked as a nurse at a retirement home and as a caregiver at a home for special kids. She could be called in at any moment and might have had to leave urgently. It wasn't completely unusual.

What was unusual was seeing a kaba'a-wearing Auntie Estella enter the gym with the female coach much later in the day while Belinda stood in line for cheerleader tryouts. She had been nervous, scared of making a fool of herself and ruining the fastest way of becoming a cool kid but that changed when she saw Auntie Estella. Her nervousness became full-blown alarm. She knew something was wrong. Belinda had thought of accidents but refused to consider death. How could she have even thought of death when Auntie Estella had just said, "We need to go to the hospital right away"?

When they finally got to the hospital, rather than rush to her mother's sickbed as she'd expected, they went directly to a doctor's office, a family friend Belinda

recognised. Without an explanation, Belinda was asked to
show her arm for a syringe. Belinda had several questions to
ask, but Auntie Estella's pleading eyes encouraged her to
obey first, in this instance. Auntie Estella was her mother's
best friend and her favourite aunt. She was a big woman,
with the height to match her weight so she looked like a
female warrior. She always wore clothes with loud colours,
fuchsia and lime-green screaming against her skin the
colour of pebbe spices and just as smooth. Auntie Estella
could make Belinda's mum laugh even when she seemed
furious and Auntie Estella gave her the coolest birthday
gifts. That is why despite the apprehension she felt, she sat
there collected, if not calm, as they tested her for HIV
without her knowing. In the future, Belinda would often
wonder what she would have done had she known that she
was being tested for HIV because her mum had just died
from shock at the news that she had it.

But at that time Belinda had not known, so she had
waited for her results in ignorance, her mind preoccupied
with imagining what state her mother was in if a doctor was
here taking her blood, her mouth busy chomping on the
sweets set out for grabs on the waiting-room table.

They didn't wait long. The doctor friend called Auntie
Estella aside and gave her the results in private. Belinda only
saw her return with a tear-streaked face, her arms opening
wide for Belinda to enter. Auntie Estella's hug was tight,
she mumbled repeatedly, "You are okay, thank God he
spared you, and you are okay." Belinda had felt good
enough to ask the questions on her mind then: "Then why
are you crying, where is mummy, can we visit her even if

she has the flu? Is she in another room here?" She was only given answers later, after returning home and eating the fast food they'd bought on the way. Auntie Estella spoke as if she was telling a story of someone else's life. She called her mum by her first name, rather than saying "your mother". She said, "Beatrice had a heart failure after getting some bad news." She did not tell Belinda what sort of news had induced heart failure, nor that heart failure equalled death. When Belinda asked more questions, she was told that they would all find out more later. But she, Auntie Estella said, will be with her all through. So, Belinda was left to put her active imagination to use. Nothing she imagined could be close to the truth.

She couldn't have imagined that her father had travelled two weeks ago without telling them that he had been diagnosed with AIDS, which was why he had gone back to Cameroon with the idea of being cured by a certain Man of God. She couldn't have imagined that her father who had gone looking for a way to be healed was discovered by his cousins who had called her mum and yelled at her, accusing her of infecting their brother. She couldn't have imagined that the reason she hadn't seen her mother that morning was because Beatrice had decided to bravely go alone to the local clinic and get tested. Despite her active imagination, Belinda could never have imagined that her mother, learning she was HIV positive, had decided to take a walk in the park and clear her head. Belinda could never have imagined that it was as she walked alone at a park not too far from Belinda's school, thinking of how to share this news with her daughter, fearing her daughter was also infected, that Beatrice Achu's heart gave out, failed from struggling to contain both her pain and what she imagined her only daughter would feel.

Belinda couldn't have imagined all this, but she would find out in the following weeks that this could be. And it had happened.

The proof of it was that she was here in Bamenda in December and there was no snow on the brink of Christmas. For the first time in as long as she could remember she wouldn't have a white Christmas, nor would she have her parents.

As Belinda slept drenched in her memories, Ameh marched to the room ready to give her a good yelling, and possibly twist her ears. It was Belinda's duty to clean up the kitchen after Ameh and Bih had cooked, but she kept avoiding it. They were all dependents on Mami and Pa now and Belinda had to learn that. Yes, she may be the direct grandchild arriving from America while Ameh and Bih were the grandnieces brought in from the village, but as long as she ate and slept in this house she had to do her share. Washing the dishes was a minor chore, but the girl always had an excuse to escape. Yesterday, it was because she had gone to the cybercafé and lost track of time, before that, she was on her menses and had cramps—as if cramps ever stopped life from happening

Immediately Ameh entered the room she felt something was wrong. The *madame* was sleeping, but fitfully; her head tossing from side to side, her fists gripping the bedspread. Ameh looked Belinda over, took in the signature short hair of a boarding student, her nice shade of brown—the colour of bitter kola before the shell was cracked—and the tear tracks on her face which lent a back story to the fitful sleep. Ameh hesitated, perhaps she shouldn't get the child up for a scolding. It could wait. It was then her eyes landed on the note, pinned down with the Advil bottle serving as a paperweight. She read the note once, then twice, then after her eyes had scanned the measly three sentences for the third time, she heard herself exclaim, "Jesus!" even though she felt speechless.

"Get up! Get up!" Ameh was pounding on Belinda's body now, willing God to let her live just so she could kill her. That is how Belinda came "back to life," with Ameh's fists drumming on her chests and Ameh's voice breaking in half sobs over her name and the constant repetition of "Jesus, Jesus, God abeg!" Belinda coughed and sputtered and opened her eyes even as Ameh commanded for her to do just that.

Resigned to the knowledge that she was still very much alive, Belinda drew herself up on the bed, hugging herself with her arms folded to her chest. The first thing she realised was that she had a headache. One would think that after taking fifteen ibuprofen tablets one would at least be void of a headache. Her hand went up to wipe her eyes and she felt her still tear-damp eyelashes which could explain the headache.

Belinda gradually took in Ameh's presence, feeling the callouses of Ameh's hands on her arms as she willed Belinda's attention, demanding obvious answers to her questions: "Who wrote this note? What did you mean? Get up, answer me! Are you mad?"

"Leave me alone. Why did you wake me up?" Belinda's voice was low and drawn out. "You should have just left me."

"You are mad. You must be!" Ameh spoke with surprising rage for someone who had just been begging God for Belinda's life. "Or whether na curse for this family oh? God forbid!" She snapped her fingers as if warding off the imagined curse and continued in an obvious attempt to backtrack, "See eh, if you wan die, please do it when I have left this house because me I don't want to have to work for another funeral. Nonsense!"

When Ameh suddenly got up and left, Belinda feared what would come next. Feared what her grandparents' reactions would be; Pa was already weak from losing so much and Mami would surely take her to the Pentecostal church she now frequented for an exorcism.

But Ameh didn't tell Mami or Pa; she didn't even bring up the incident. She was noticeably nicer though; she didn't scold Belinda so much and must have asked Bih not to as well. It was three days later when Ameh finally did approach her. It was a Saturday so Bih had gone to the market and Pa and Mami had gone to play njangi. Only the two of them were left at home.

Ameh met Belinda in the bedroom the girls shared. She sounded uncomfortable as she asked Belinda to sit up. "I want to talk with you," she said. "About what you did the other day." Belinda said nothing, just waited to hear what she'd been expecting, a scolding and that her grandparents must be told.

"I have not told Mami or Pa because it would be too much for them just now. But I hope you know that what you did was wrong. I hope you know."

Belinda knew no such thing. But still said nothing.

Ameh continued, "I have been thinking of how to discuss what must have pushed you to think of such a thing." Belinda noted that Ameh obviously found it difficult to say suicide. "I know you have had a very difficult time, but I think you are more blessed than you realise."

Belinda felt her eyes sting. She wanted to cry and was struggling not to in Ameh's presence. Whether Ameh noticed the struggle or not, she continued speaking calmly. "I asked a friend of mine about this," and as Belinda lowered her head in frustration, Ameh added quickly, "I didn't mention that it was you, and he's not even in Cameroon. I just asked him how to help someone like you." Belinda heard "someone suicidal" clearly. "He said some things, a lot. And he reminded me of a film we had watched together when he was in Cameroon, *Freedom Writers*. I watched it again yesterday. We can watch it together if you like. But it gave me this idea I hope will help."

Ameh moved from the door where she'd been leaning and speaking all this while and Belinda raised her head as she approached, noticing a book in her hand for the first time.

"Take this ledger, I want you to use it as a journal. If you can't talk to me just write what is disturbing you in the book and leave it in the brown handbag under the bed. No one touches it. We'll be the only ones to use the journal. I'll occasionally write prompts for you to think about in it, like exercises. My friend gave me some. And you can answer as you like."

Ameh stopped talking for a while, likely out of exasperation over Belinda's silence. When she opened her mouth again, her words were a tired plea. "I don't want to tell Mami or Pa about this, I want to understand and help. Please Belinda, I beg you, please don't think of taking your life. Please just try this journal thing and help me help you, okay? Please?"

The tears Belinda had been struggling with fell freely now. Ameh joined her on the bed and hugged her, now the silent one as Belinda's heavy sobs echoed through the otherwise empty house.

This is how Ameh became an amateur therapist; regularly visiting the cybercafé to seek knowledge from her former ENS classmate now furthering his studies as a counsellor in the US, all in an attempt to help Belinda overcome what neither of them understood.

In the weeks that followed they had whole conversations through the journal. And as Belinda returned to the dormitory with the resumption of school, Ameh would visit on Fridays. One of the on-campus staff was a family friend and they would meet there for "journal handovers." One journal became two, then four by the next holiday.

Belinda would make an entry in the journal with some problem that weighed her down; whether or not to forgive her father and if so how? Why she had to stay with Mami and Pa even though they hardly made any effort to understand her, to understand that she was different. Or some soliloquy of discontent; her dreams of how her sweet sixteen would be, her thoughts on boarding school and how it meant living with bullies in school and having no escape… she would prefer to attend a day school.

After every entry, using a different colour pen, blue or red in contrast to Belinda's preferred black, Ameh would make inserts here or there as if reviewing Belinda's train of thought, finding the negativity, attacking its one-sided logic and suggesting another perspective. With her red pen, Ameh would correct Belinda's perception of herself:

No, you are not ugly with your low hair. You look like a student should, and you are beautiful, see your white neat teeth; your skin is so pretty, I envy it; your eyes are like Aunty Beatrice's own and Pa always smiles because of them.

In one entry Belinda had ranted over being maltreated by Mami and Pa who were miserly with the things which had been shipped for Belinda after the sale of her parents' home in the US. She railed over being forced to live in Cameroon when she had an American nationality, raged over not even having a good allowance like the other kids in her school whose parents were in the US.

Belinda received the journal the following Sunday to see a two-page entry from Ameh in blue pen offering insights that Belinda had missed or what Pa and Mami, had, in part-kindness and part-adult patronising, deemed unnecessary to tell her.

It was Ameh who told her that most of her parents' savings had been used up between her father's impromptu trip to Cameroon, and her mother's death and subsequent shipping of her corpse home. Ameh had informed her that her father's story had made rounds in Buea, where he was based, and the shop he had set up was doing poorly as people still had a stigma against AIDS patients. He was barely able to support his treatment let alone contribute to providing for Belinda. He had been asked to return to the US but so far seemed to prefer hopelessly waiting on what would eventually happen.

Ameh's entry also informed Belinda that the house she had lived in with her parents was foreclosed upon and that the stuff she had in barrels were the last she may ever have, so Mami and Pa were only trying to make them last. Aunty Estella had sent the barrels, Ameh wrote, she had struggled to pack her personal belongings, selling what she could and buying any amenities she felt Belinda and her grandparents would need in Cameroon—things she had seen Belinda's mum buy before. Few of Belinda's parents' friends had helped beyond funeral contributions, Junior's mother being one of the few to send clothes for Belinda.

There was no money, Ameh told her; Mami and Pa were dependent on the rents they received from their tenants in the set of rooms they had built decades ago on land leading up to the village. This source of income had been ameliorated by what Belinda's mother would regularly send home and the sporadic payment of their pensions by the government insurance fund, CNPS.

Ameh ended that entry sternly. Belinda, she said, ought to come to terms with the new reality. She had little, and ought to be grateful for people like Aunty Estella who were helping, be grateful to Mami and Pa who were trying their best with the little they had.

After that entry, Belinda did not write the following week. More than ever, she felt like a burden and wanted to die. Perhaps Ameh had sensed it, perhaps she just thought she had to do something to keep the journal exchange going. Whatever the reason, journal entries thereafter were led by Ameh who forced Belinda to write with "homework," or wrote her own messages to Belinda for her to just read or respond to.

Belinda would collect the journal and see "write five things you hate about your life and find five things you like" written in red ink. Belinda would write seven things she hated and listing Ameh, Aunty Estella and Junior as the only good. Ameh would start a list titled: "Belinda's Reasons to Live" and keep pages folded after the list pages, explaining with an asterisk at the bottom that the reasons will keep coming to them so they should leave room for more.

B

Belinda thought about all this on the flight to Cameroon. She had returned to the US as soon as she made the A' Levels and had returned only twice to Cameroon since then: once for her grandfather's funeral and once for Ameh's marriage. Ameh had saved her, given her a sense of purpose, and inspired her decision to study clinical psychology and help others choose life again, as she had been helped.

She thought of Ameh regularly, of her offering therapy with no training, just love and will. But till now, all these years later, Belinda was only just realising that Ameh never showed her own pain. Why hadn't she ever left a blank journal page for Ameh to share what disturbed her? Why hadn't she ever returned the favour as an adult? How could she have thought bimonthly calls and gifts of money for birthdays and Christmas were enough? She had believed Ameh was content as an ENS graduate, a government school teacher with a fairly regular pay, a husband and beautiful daughter. A belief that was shattered just two days ago with news of Ameh hospitalised and on life support after what was reported as the latest of regular battering at the hands of her husband.

Restless in her seat, Belinda tried to picture an abused Ameh and clenched her fists. Was this too not attempting suicide in a different way, to stay in a relationship suffocating you? Had Ameh ever written a note, mentioned something that could have been an SOS? Nothing came to mind. But like Ameh had done over a decade before when she found Belinda's note, Belinda whispered the two-word prayer, "God abeg." With those two words Belinda willed the flight to arrive in time, hoped she was not too late, that Ameh was still alive, and pleaded for a second chance for the person who had helped her live again.

BRRRRRRRRRRRRRRRRR!

A. Bouna Guazong

Translated from the French by Hannah Jakobsen

Bam! The back door of the taxi slammed shut. Taking off like Usain Bolt, Champion set off on the tortuous two-hundred-metre path that separated the pavement from his home in the swamp at the bottom of the hill.

"Sir, your money! Sir…" the driver yelled in vain after looking left and right. Champion had already vanished into Obili's ghetto. Barely fifty metres in, he turned to acrobatics to dodge a motorcycle taxi. For once, that day, God was on his side. But some fifty metres farther, he found himself lying motionless in a stranger's living room, having entered not through the door or window. He had crashed through the old, wooden wall, propelled like one of Van Helsing's arrows by a collision with another motorcycle taxi. This time, God was distracted, as He had been since the morning of that Wednesday in April. As passers-by yelled and rushed over, the young man stayed unmoving, his eyes wide open. Then, blood slowly began to drip from his ears, mouth, and nose. The young Kulu Ybaning, more commonly known as Champion, a twenty-six-year-old graduate with a BSc in Chemistry, unemployed full-time, flew his white flag. He had lost the war of life. The train of his dreams and ambitions had just pulled into its ultimate station.

It was a Wednesday evening in April. Champion left the Ministry of Public Service completely disoriented, and in a rush. For the past eight months, he had frequented their Human Resources department to enquire about the application he had submitted two years earlier. He hadn't submitted the application because the ministry was recruiting, but rather for the simple reason that the director of the ministry's HR department lived not far from his neighbourhood. The paths of the two men had crossed multiple times, one always in his BMW, the other always on the heel-toe express. However, the first and only time they met face-to-face, things didn't go the way Champion had planned.

The events that follow are not recounted in real time, talk less of in chronological order, but it all started with his graduation from high school.

Up to his graduation, Kulu Ybaning did not have a nickname. Then, in the university, as he experienced the social realities of Kamer, Kulu ended up going by the moniker "Champion." He chose this nickname simply because he believed that a name bore influence on personality especially as his names, which literally meant "poor tortoise" when combined, weren't bringing him any luck. He therefore thought it fair to take on a well-boding nickname to triumph over life, one that could boost him into action whenever he looked at himself in the mirror: Champion. He had opted for "Champion" because he wished to be one. Having been born into a poor family, into destitution, he *had* to be a champion to make it in Kamer. Besides, nicknames were a common phenomenon; the official name of the country itself was not Kamer, nor was Ongola the official name of the political capital where he lived. In fact, he lived in a country where reality was akin to fiction, a film straight out of Hollywood.

He was barely 1.8 metres tall, a handsome and elegant young man who tried, as much as his limited resources could allow, to dress as stylishly as his contemporaries did.

Financially speaking, he was not of the middle class but way below it. In short, he was a young, childless, unemployed bachelor with no prospects for the future. He was the son of a poor man in a country where social status tended to be hereditary; the sons of the unemployed were unemployed, the sons of ministers ended up becoming ministers. To make things worse, Champion was a two-time orphan: his father and his mother. His father had died one Wednesday in April when Champion was nine years old, after a brief, scientifically inexplicable, illness. His mother, for her part, died when he was twenty years old, on another Wednesday in April. She had been diagnosed with a benign tumour, but the operation went south. This type of thing was normal in hospitals in Kamer, where patients receive prognoses in the place of diagnoses. And when, by chance, the diagnosis is correct, you're still not off the hook because instead of surgeons we have butchers.

Thus, as both of his parents had died on a Wednesday, Champion had a particular relationship with Wednesdays, especially those in April. The only good thing ever to have occurred in his life on a Wednesday was his degree—he received it on a Wednesday after six years in the Faculty of Science at the University of Yaounde I. But that was the same Wednesday he learned that he wouldn't be able to continue his studies because a new university regulation had been put out. The regulation, enacted for the sole purpose of expelling those students who were frustrated by the system and thus more likely to rebel, stipulated the following: *Any student who has taken longer than four years to complete a Bachelor's Degree should kindly turn to a private university to prove their mettle (if any) as students.* Therefore, on the very Wednesday that Champion became a graduate in Chemical Sciences, he joined the ranks of the unemployed, full time. Private universities were too expensive for poor parents, therefore out of the reach of HIPOs: Heavily Indebted Poor Orphans. With this new status, Champion lived his life peacefully, busying himself with the search for a job to solve his problems. And problems he certainly had plenty of. Little did he know there were more to come.

Of all the illnesses the good Lord invited on Earth to upset the calm that comes with being in good health, diarrhoea deserves a place of honour. The problem that comes along with diarrhoea is that you're forced to rush to the restroom whether you want to or not, whenever the malady decides. But, in contrast to HIV, tuberculosis, a cough, or anything else, diarrhoea comes with a virtue as well: courage. Truly! He who is afflicted with diarrhoea fears nothing. Ongola, the capital of Kamer, is a city where insecurity is a reality. Past a certain hour, it's best not to venture outdoors—even on one's own veranda! Especially in ghettos like Obili, where Champion lived. But two Wednesdays had gone by since Champion had started spending almost every night on his veranda. Where was he getting this courage from? From a case of chronic and rebellious diarrhoea, considering that the hostel's toilet was not in his room but at the end of the building.

The morning of that Wednesday, as five hours had passed since his last trip to the toilet, he thought the tablets he had picked up on credit from the storekeeper across the street had overcome his ailment. He then recalled that, on the last Wednesday he had been at the Ministry, the secretary had asked him not to return for at least a month. He would have remembered it anyway, because since the Wednesday of the previous week, his girlfriend hadn't for one minute stopped asking him for money for her upcoming childbirth—money which he, of course, didn't have. In any case, when you've got yourself a woman, a pregnant woman, a nine-month-pregnant woman, a nine-month-pregnant woman with certain whims, a nine-months-pregnant-woman with the whims of a nine-month-pregnant woman and who wants money, you can't forget to leave for a job interview despite any chronic diarrhoea. So even if the storekeeper's pills had done nothing for him, Champion would get himself to the Ministry that Wednesday; he didn't have a choice.

A proverb has it that it is during your wife's first pregnancy that you miss bachelorhood. After putting on his Sunday best, Champion decided to stop by his girlfriend's house, so that he might prove to her, if it were still necessary to do so, that he wasn't deaf to her complaints and that he was struggling to better their lives. Eh! That Wednesday, he judged it preferable to go directly to see his girlfriend for the bickering—instead of calling and getting scolded over the phone—so that he could gain some time. Besides, he couldn't call because his neighbourhood had not had power for two days and his phone was holding on to not more than one bar of battery.

As he could not make a phone call and risk completely depleting his battery, potentially missing a call from the ministry, it was naturally more sensible to make the trip and be lectured in person without a telecoms operator acting as intermediary. However, in the end, he realized that it would have been better to call her and deplete his battery. By the time he was leaving his girlfriend's place, Champion wasn't heading to the ministry simply because he wanted a job. He was now heading there in pursuit of a means to cause his girlfriend to hurt, a means of revenge. It is a feeling that is common in love relationships, seeking revenge on one's partner after being jilted when one still feels for the said partner. While men try to find a woman who is prettier and smarter than their ex, women tend to seek a man who is richer than their ex or even hope that their ex doesn't become successful, so that they don't regret anything. So, Champion was now heading to the ministry to find a job that would give him a high status, the type of social status that makes some women dream. Yet, for the record, Champion had not left his girlfriend's place in that state of mind because she had left him, no—It was worse. She was nine months pregnant. Not only had she left him, but she had also announced that, just after the child's birth, she would be getting married... to someone else. He therefore thought that if he became a civil servant at the ministry, she would regret dumping him.

That Wednesday morning, Champion was prepared for a lot when he got to his girlfriend's house: a bad mood, insults, insolence... but not a "divorce." For more than a week, his girlfriend had harassed him day and night to cough up the money needed for the birth. Why would a woman who knows her boyfriend to be a jobless graduate put such pressure on him for this money? Simply because in this country's hospitals there's an advanced childbirth technique for those without money: self-service. It simply entails going to a pharmacy, picking up scalpels and anything you think might be useful, setting up the expectant mother on a lawn or even on the ground on the premises of the hospital, and playing doctor or nurse yourself! In short, in Kamer, the public health system has instituted self-service for the poor. When you don't have money, you diagnose yourself, prescribe yourself medicine, buy it yourself over the counter and off you go! Whatever happens, happens. This service hadn't bothered anyone until the day when a woman lost her sister and her two babies while trying to perform a caesarean on the lawn of a major hospital. Upon the tragic death of Monique and her twin babies, all pregnant women understood that if you're heading to a hospital for childbirth or prenatal care, it's best to have money if you want to be sure to leave the place alive.

But upon arriving at her house, he was surprised to find his girlfriend calm, happy even.

"Hello darling, I wanted—" he'd started.

"Dar- what? Who's your darling?" she'd cut in.

"Listen, I know that—"

"You don't know anything, you're no Socrates."

"I mean… I'm on my way to the ministry for my appointment…"

"What do I care?"

Until that point, Champion had dismissed her attitude as the impulses of a nine-month-pregnant woman. He couldn't have been further from the truth.

"Listen I know you're upset with...."

"Up- what...? Do I look upset? My friend, give me a break. This nightmare with you is over. In two weeks, that is next Wednesday, my fiancé will be here. Please, if you love me as you claim, stop coming for me. I'm getting married and the last I checked, you are not my fiancé. So, you and I are finished."

"Are you joking or what?"

"Excuse me, they're waiting for you at the ministry; don't let me make you late."

"Hey girl, your phone's ringing, it's that white man of yours," yelled a voice from inside the house, and Champion's girlfriend went back inside, leaving him alone on the veranda. Like so many other girls, she had found herself a white man. Champion stayed outside alone for 30 minutes, resolving to leave only when the living room door slammed shut and startled him. His brain had crashed, like that of an actor who forgets his lines in the middle of a performance. As a comedian used to say, "To a woman, when you have money, you're the love of her life. When you're poor, you're the bane of her existence." So, it was with a brain that had just lost its capacities for logical thought that Champion decided to continue on his way to the ministry to check up on his application, probably telling himself, "if I get the job, she'll regret this."

One often hears that a woman is a necessary evil, but believe me, if that was true, God would have one. Instead, he bestowed his son upon the wife of a certain Joseph, and then left her to her husband. Women then, aren't they only useful in procreation? If Champion could speak from beyond the grave, he would certainly answer "yes." The worst thing that can happen to a man is not to fall in love, but to love a woman who is not worth the trouble. And that, Champion learned the hard way. In his first year at university, he fell in love with a woman and when he made love to her for the first time, it was a Wednesday in April. And if he always remembered that date, it's not because it was a Wednesday in April, but rather because it was the first time he was infected with gonorrhoea. After that experience, he swore to never again concern himself with beautiful women and never again fall in love. For two years, he followed that plan. Eventually, he got to the third year of his chemistry programme, after almost six years at university...

Regarding the six years, Champion was not a bad student; he graduated from high school on time, and with a B-plus average which was not common in the 2000s. It took him six years to finish his university programme for two reasons. The first is that, like many young people of his social class at that time, he went to university and continued to study to see if he could figure out something else to do with his life. Second, the teaching methodology at the University of Yaounde I, and particularly at the Faculty of Science where Champion studied, was not exactly conducive for the intellectual development of a genius. How could it be when, for just one course, for example, an amphitheatre with a capacity of 1,000 and no audio equipment ends up with a minimum 1,500 students per lecture?

Anyway, as a third-year chemistry student, he fell deeply in love with Elise, the girl who'd ditch him for a white man. Elise! What a beauty! Her only fault was that you would've been hard-pressed to find a fault in her. Naaaah! That woman, she was good. Always smiling, friendly. She was beautiful, even when you looked at her face with the sun behind her back, because her smile and beautiful white teeth didn't go unnoticed. She didn't need more than two hours of conversation with you to give you the impression that you'd known each other for two years. She was very approachable; maybe even a bit too much so. Elise was so beautiful that Champion would often blaspheme by saying that, considering that Jesus has promised to return, if now were the time, Elise would be the one to take on Mary's role. Elise! Have you ever met someone you couldn't find a serious fault in even after several years? A wise man once said, to succeed in love, find a woman you would like to sleep with the rest of your life, a woman with personality, and a woman who loves you unconditionally, but, most importantly, make sure those three women never meet. Champion knew this, but with Elise, he thought he had outsmarted probability because, as he often said on the subject, Elise was a combination of the three in one. She had character, she loved him unconditionally, and he wished to sleep with her the rest of his life. Elise, a student like him, never sought his help with any serious financial problem, which Champion found romantic and sometimes boasted about. Everything was working perfectly with Elise, so much so that it was suspicious, troubling, and fishy. Especially as the very first time Champion had met her was on one Wednesday afternoon in April, and she told him "yes" the following Wednesday... The healthiness of this relationship was therefore a cause for concern since, throughout all his life, he had never had a good history with Wednesdays. That was then...

So, Champion set off to the ministry from his girlfriend's, still in his Sunday best. Elise had given him a sizeable appetizer, but he knew that the main course would be getting past the ministry's security. To get by a guard at the entrance of a building in Kamer, a public building for that matter, was anything but simple. Getting by a guard had gotten so complicated that, had Jesus lived today, he'd say, "It's tougher for a rich man to enter the kingdom of heaven than for a man to get past a guard in front of a government building." To get past a guard, one had to answer questions such as, "Who are you?", "Where are you going?", "Who sent you?", "...what for?", "When?" and "Who told you could enter here just like that?"... The purpose of this exercise is not to help you with directions, but rather to disorientate you such that you end up having to supplement their monthly income before being let in. After the guard's test, which he passed thanks to the number of times he'd been through the drill, Champion sighed and took a deep breath, thinking that the day's obstacles were over and that he couldn't come up against anything worse, not after what had happened with Elise. But no, there was even more to come.

His head completely in the clouds, Champion headed towards the elevator. After pressing the button multiple times with no response, he noticed that he was the only one trying to use the elevator and that everyone was looking at him with puzzled expressions on their faces. Then he realized that the only elevator that worked was the minister's. The visitors' elevator had broken down. In spite of himself, he took the stairs to get to the tenth floor where HR was located. Given his condition, he first made the sign of the cross, then started on the stairs. He crossed the first floor, then the second, then the third, and so on until the tenth floor without needing to run to the restroom.

"Bonjour Madame," he said to the secretary.

"You again?" responded the young woman, irritated.

"Bonjour Mademoiselle," Champion corrected himself.

"The director is here, but I don't know if he'll see you today. Have a seat and wait a little if you have time…"

From her tone, he understood that the ellipsis that trailed the end of her sentence spelled out clearly that she meant "…if you have time to lose." So Champion, having nothing left to lose except time, took a seat.

Sitting in the waiting area, Champion thought he had pulled through it all, so much so that he even found himself looking up and smiling from time to time at the young secretary, who looked at him with disdain. But had he? When a university graduate in full possession of all his mental faculties chooses to buy his medication from a shop, what is he really thinking? That a pharmacy sells cookies?

One thing about diarrhoea is that there is some advice that doesn't need to come from a prescription to be valid because it always turns out to be useful. For example, one is advised to wear loose clothing that doesn't take more than a second to take off... But Champion had forgotten that one and had donned his nice suit, probably because he thought he was off the hook.

The events that follow occur between 10 am and 4 pm.

Champion was calmly seated when, out of a sudden, like an earthquake that was 2.3 in magnitude on the Richter scale, a preliminary tremor rocked his body, starting from his intestines, and coursing through his stomach up to his head. Then a second tremor of the same magnitude, then a third, then a fourth of 8.8 in magnitude. His teeth ground together, his cheeks hollowed, his nostrils flared, and his eyes bulged wide, as he looked left, right, right, left.

"Everything alright, sir?" asked the secretary.

In spite of himself, Champion smiled, nodding. But the tremors didn't stop. So, after making the sign of the cross twice, he got up. When you have diarrhoea and the time to go to the toilet comes, even the good Lord can't help you. Why, then, did Champion make the sign of the cross? Because, in Kamer, finding an open public restroom in a public building is like finding Nicolas Sarkozy and Dominique de Villepin sitting around a table and laughing hysterically in 2008 or 2009.

"Is there a problem, sir?" pushed the secretary.

"Toi-let," pronounced Champion, with great difficulty.

"Go towards the left, second hallway, first door on your right," the secretary told him.

"Thank you, Madame."

"Mademoiselle," the secretary repeated, with anger and condescension.

"Ah! Mademoiselle!" Champion corrected himself as he picked up his cell phone and headed in the direction of the door to the hallway.

"Hey! It's on the second floor," she added.

"What?"

"The bathroom for visitors is on the second floor."

"Down there?"

"Obviously, we're on the tenth. Or is the tenth below the second in your universe?"

Champion knew very well how to count and that two is below ten. However, he was unsettled by the thought that he had to go down eight flights of stairs with an urgent diarrhoea making its way towards his bottom. The only shortcut to get down faster would be to jump down, but jump how and to get where exactly? Champion, haunches squeezed together, holding his pants tightly with his two hands, took to the stairs; first with small steps, then with little jumps, his legs clasped together. As things weren't going so well in his stomach, he thought for a moment about laying down on the floor and rolling on his stomach. Instead, he increased the pace of his jumps while keeping his legs clasped tightly. It was a spectacle indeed to watch him go down the stairs. The few cultivated people amongst the visitors at the ministry even thought it was a performance art piece. It had all the trappings of the genre: apprehension, absurdity, lack of artistic process. In short, it was a spiritual masturbation, just like philosophy in modern times.

In the end, after more than a dozen minutes of a surrealist spectacle as incomprehensible as contemporary dance, Champion finally arrived at the visitors' restroom. He had just entered and was undoing his belt when it went Brrrrrrrrrrrr! in his pants. Too late, the damage was done. He pulled down the pants, sat on the toilet and Brrrrrrrrrrrrrrrrrr some more, freely. Forty minutes later he was still sitting on the toilet, Brrrrrrrrrrrrrrrrrrrr, when his telephone rang. The ministry's number appeared, and Champion picked up immediately without thinking.

"Hello," he answered the call, with a voice as morbid as a zombie's.

"Sir, the director wants to see you in five minutes, and he's stepping out for an emergency," the voice of the secretary on the phone informed him.

"Yes, I'm coming, right away," replied Champion without thinking.

The secretary hung up and it was then that Champion realized that he shouldn't have picked up so quickly. However, even if he had taken the time to think, what would he have done? To land a job interview with a director when you're not from the same family is all but unheard of in Kamer. Champion knew this, but to go to an interview with some Brrrrrrrrrrrr in your pants, you must be from another planet or have strange intentions. But there was something pushing Champion: if he left without meeting the director, how would he get his revenge on Elise who had humiliated him that morning about the advanced depletion of his pockets? It was in that moment that Champion understood that, of all things man had invented, toilet paper was the most important. Ah! Toilet paper, or TP as it is widely referred to, was what he needed. He looked up, down, right, left, nothing. The ministry's restrooms had never seen a trace of TP. To top it all, there was no water. The poor guy grabbed his courage with both hands, put on his pants, and started, soaring, up the stairs.

When he arrived at the ninth floor his phone rang again and, while still running, he picked up, put it to his ear and yelled, "I'm just around the corner, right here!" But as he couldn't hear a reply, he stopped and looked at the screen; it was a text. As physical exercise was not his forte, he took the opportunity catch his breath. He kept climbing slowly while reading the text, then stopped dead in his tracks, eyes fixed on the screen of his phone: "Elise gave birth, but there is a problem. It's best if you don't come." He didn't recognize the number, so he tried to call it, but the battery that hadn't stopped flashing all the while had finally died, and the phone was off. Consumed with anger and shaking, he lost his grip on the telephone, which flew downward from the ninth floor and the only thing he heard was the bang of it hitting the railings of the stairs, then the final sound of it hitting the floor on the ground level.

Champion took a breath and remembered that the director was going to leave in thirty seconds, so he doubled his speed and found himself face-to-face with the director in the secretary's office. Once in the office, Champion understood that nothing good could ever befall him on a Wednesday. As soon as he entered, the secretary turned on the fan that was just behind him to maximum power. The gas of mass destruction hit the director smack in the face, stinging his nostrils.

"You, out!" screamed the director.

"S- sir, I…" Champion stammered.

"I said outside!"

"I… I…"

"Outside! Learn to have a little shame in this country!"

He had chosen to go by the nickname "Champion" so it could boost his morale when he was feeling depressed, but this was more than he could take. He had a chronic and rebellious diarrhoea, he had just lost another job opportunity and, worse, he had no idea if he was now a father or not. That Wednesday evening in April, Champion burst out of the Ministry of Public Service completely disoriented.

After a stop at his house to change, Champion, who still didn't know who had sent him the text, ran to the clinic where Elise went for antenatal care. When he arrived the room in question, his baby was in a crib and healthy, but to his surprise, it was of mixed-race. Elise, daughter of a black father and a black mother, had a mixed-race baby with a black man? Eh! As would be said in Kamer, she had "pressed 'spoil'".

"So, all this time you weren't pregnant with my child?" he asked Elise.

"You should be thanking God that he's not yours. Can you take care of a child?" Elise responded coldly.

"Do you know how much your baby stuff and your pregnancy all cost me?"

"Hold it! You can calculate it and I'll reimburse you as soon as my husband comes. And I'll pay you in euros, if you don't mind…"

"It's him, isn't it?"

"Please, leave me alone. I didn't call you here."

Champion gave Elise two slaps so strong that she collapsed, yelling. This attracted the attention of the guards, who gave him a good beating before bothering to find out what had happened. They believed Elise when she said he was just a thug who was confusing her with some other girl. Which was more or less believable because she had given birth to a mixed-race child and Champion, not being her brother, could only be a stranger because it was even less probable that he could be the baby's father.

Champion left the hospital, stumbling. He realized why and how his girlfriend had given birth to a mixed-race baby. In the second semester of the third year of his Bachelor's Degree, Champion had put up a white man named Emile Detrop. Detrop was a friend of a cousin of his who was in Europe, and he had come to Cameroon for an academic internship. Over time, he had become one person too many in Champion's private life. Champion had become accustomed to often finding Elise and this Detrop together at his house, but as Elise was a very nice and approachable girl, he never grew suspicious. Now, Champion understood that Elise not asking him for money too often was anything but a romantic gesture. It was because Detrop was providing for her, maybe a little too much even. Champion started recalling a plethora of things that had seemed trivial at the time but were rather revealing when it concerned

Elise's love. Indeed, she had started falling "head over heels" for him only when she found out that he had a cousin in Europe with whom he was on rather good terms. He could now understand the real reason why Elise had been harassing him to ask his cousin to help him emigrate from Kamer. All she'd wanted was to have a boyfriend in Europe, to go there, or even get the Holy Grail: a white husband. She was "just trying to find her own white man," which was the common trend as people sought to have a direct relationship with a person living in Europe—in the euro zone. Achieving this was tantamount to automatically changing one's social standing. As a comedian put it, "blessed are those who have a cousin in Europe for, sooner or later, they shall see the colour of euros, even if the cousin is a zero." After all, the exchange rate for 1 euro was 650 CFA francs, which was enough money for one's needs on an ordinary day. Elise was no different from all the other girls in Kamer; she had finally found her white man.

The events that follow occur from 4 pm local time, on a Wednesday evening in April.

Champion set off on his way home. It was evening and Ongola was readying itself for its daily 5 pm traffic jams. A taxi rolled calmly towards Obili. The driver turned towards Champion, alone in the back.

"You sure everything's fine, sir? You seem rather restless for a normal man."

"It's fine," replied Champion, handing a 1,000-franc bill to the driver.

As the latter bent over to get the change, he heard two successive Brrrrrrrrrrrrrrrrrrrr's, and by the time he sat back up Champion had already disappeared into the neighbourhood. Taking off like Usain Bolt, the young man set off on the tortuous two-hundred-metre path that separates the pavement from his place in the swamp at the bottom of the hill.

ℬ

Elise did not attend Champion's burial.

She had always known that Champion wasn't the father of her unborn child. However, as Emile Detrop had cut off contact with her after returning to his country, she had fallen back on Champion. That is, until the day she heard from Emile Detrop when she was in her ninth month of pregnancy, only a few days before the birth. It appeared that Detrop had finally convinced his parents that he wanted to marry an African woman who was pregnant with his child. Emile Detrop arrived in the country, married his beloved, and the two left for Europe, then Asia for their honeymoon. Coming back from Malaysia, they took Malaysia Airlines, flight MH370, a flight that never landed.

BAD LAKE

Nkiacha Atemnkeng

François and his two colleagues, Fondzenyuy and Murphy, stared at the gas siphoning system installed in Lake Nyos with excitement. Two very long polyethylene pipes set up vertically from the bottom of the lake to its surface emerged in the middle of a floating raft, on which the scientists stood. They wore gas masks, life jackets and boots.

"Are we ready to launch it?" François asked.

"Yes, the equipment is ready," Fondzenyuy confirmed.

"It's D-Day. You look a little nervous, Docteur François," whispered Murphy, as the French scientist pinned his gaze on the water surface.

"Murphy, c'est comme si j'ai vu quelque chose…"

"What?" Murphy asked.

"I think I saw something move on the water's surface over there," he pointed. Murphy looked, almost squinting.

"I don't see anything. Maybe it's just the sun's reflection, or you're just eager to launch so that we can be done with this tedious project," Murphy said.

François raised his voice, "Okay, on my count. Four, three, two, one, zero, initiate the process!"

Murphy pushed a button on the remote control. A buzzing drone flew upwards and mechanically unwound a pipe screw with its long spike. An automatic pump rocked back and forth. Water saturated with gas rose rapidly, entering the polyethylene pipes. The bubbles drove the gas-liquid mixture upwards, far above their heads, in a raucous frothy spray, like a fizzy drink being opened.

"Initiate!" François shouted once more. Murphy propelled the drone higher. It undid another pipe screw, triggering a second degassing of water which landed on the lake's rippling surface.

"Et pour la dernière fois!" François boomed again, pumping his right fist in the air. A third siphoning ejected a strong water jet.

"Oui!" François celebrated their achievement.

"Oh, we did it. We made history!" Murphy cheered.

"Finally, after so many years of research," Fondzenyuy beamed, switching off his video camera after filming the experiment.

"C'est incroyable. Quel exploit, et sans précédent. Le premier projet de dégazage au monde," François bluffed with peacock pride. The men embraced each other. They took off their gas masks and stepped aboard a speed boat anchored next to the raft. Murphy rode it ashore, admiring the deep, still lake situated in a circular maar high on the flank of the Oku volcanic plain. He looked up at the natural dam composed of rock which surrounded the lake's waters and remembered how they had hatched the whole grand idea.

$\mathcal{B}$

They had all heard the news via international media that a volcanic lake had exploded in the central African nation of Cameroon, suffocating hundreds of people in 1986. It had been an unheard sort of disaster, so Murphy had immediately expressed interest in investigating the lake. His university, Harvard, teamed him with the acclaimed French scientist, François Dumas, as research leaders for the project. They had both travelled to Nyos where the lake was situated. Murphy had moved about, examining the remains of the victims which offered no clues—the corpses showed no evidence of bleeding, physical trauma, or disease, and no sign of exposure to radiation, chemical weapons, or poison gas.

He had been baffled, until he stumbled upon a small clue—all the lit oil lamps in Nyos had been extinguished. François had also observed from satellite images that the lake's colour had changed from blue before the explosion to a murky reddish brown. He carried out tests and the results showed that the red on the surface was dissolved iron, normally found at the bottom of the lake. Fondzenyuy, a Cameroonian scientist who worked with them, had suggested a theory. He hypothesized that the sediment at the lake's bed had somehow been stirred up and the iron brought to the surface, where it turned to rust after being oxidized by air.

The three men had built heavily on their gas theory. They attributed the release of carbon dioxide gas not to a volcanic eruption in the lake, as there had been no seismic activity in the area, but to the active magma chamber that fed the lake's bed deep below the surface of the earth. They concluded that the lake's carbon dioxide had apparently never left its bed. Instead of bubbling to the surface like in all other lakes, it had accumulated at the bottom. An event such as a landslide had surely resulted in the rapid mixing of the supersaturated deep water with the upper layers of the lake, where the reduced compression allowed the pressurized carbon dioxide to effervesce out of the solution. It had done so in a chain reaction and had violently released a gas cloud in what they called a limnic eruption. It was that gas cloud which had enveloped Nyos, Kam, Cha and Soghum.

Murphy had later tested water samples from the lake and realized that its carbon dioxide content was rising steadily again.

"Oh no, so what do we do?" he wondered aloud.

"Firstly, we will ask the Cameroonian government to raze all the neighbouring villages at risk and relocate them far away from here," François said.

"That's a good idea," Murphy affirmed.

"Then, we will degas the lake," he added.

"Degas the lake! How's that possible? It has never been done before. That lake is two hundred metres deep!" Murphy pointed out.

"Well, before airplanes flew in the air, they first flew in the brain," François chimed, widening his confident eyes.

B

Murphy smiled and switched off the boat's engine when they reached the bank. A young intern from Nyos called Nkwain, who was working on the project, hurried towards the boat.

"Congratulations, I saw the degassing. It was impressive," he said and smiled.

"Thank you," said Murphy. Nkwain helped the men out of the boat.

"So, what is next for the project?" the intern asked.

"We need to find funding to execute it," François answered.

"So, if the degassing is done successfully, will my people be safe from another catastrophic outgassing?" Nkwain asked.

"Yes and no. We recently discovered that the northern wall of the lake is weakening. It may give way in a couple of years, releasing a lot of water and gas in a disaster which may exceed that of 1986. It can be reinforced with a lot of money and time, though," Murphy answered.

Nkwain's face fell. "Oh no!" the young man moaned.

"What?" asked Fondzenyuy.

"Our people are still resettling in the village," Nkwain said.

"So they ignored our advice not to resettle there?" Fondzenyuy asked.

"Yes."

"Did the government not raze all the villages surrounding the lake?" François was perplexed.

"That was many years ago. The villagers have gradually started returning to their land, building new houses and cultivating old farms despite our pleas," Nkwain told them.

"Est-ce que tu es sûr?" François asked.

"Oui, Docteur." François felt it was like going to sit on a toilet bowl with an alligator in it.

"I think we should go and see for ourselves then," Fondzenyuy proposed.

"Good idea," François said.

The scientists walked to the construction site where a muscular, dark-skinned man was sticking wooden poles in the earth and giving instructions. Twelve others hammered planks with nails. They had already constructed a few wooden houses.

"Good morning, my people," Fondzenyuy greeted. The men answered, barely looking back. The muscular man squinted at Fondzenyuy.

"You're…Joseph, right?" Fondzenyuy asked. "I think we met last time." The man nodded.

"My friend, I know they say there is no place like home but, as we earlier explained, Nyos is a high-risk zone. It's not advisable to continue resettling here, please."

"So what do you want us to do? Return to the camps?" Joseph asked.

"Em, yes, for now," Fondzenyuy answered.

"We are not going back to that ugly place anymore. Goment has abandoned us. We can't even farm near the camps because the soil there is not fertile. Even if it is, it is owned by other people. We are tired of waiting there with nothing to do, watching our children die of hunger, disease and neglect when our fertile ancestral lands are right here, unoccupied," Joseph reasoned, pointing towards the ground with his forefinger. The other men nodded.

"Good point, Joseph. The problem is not with the village land. It is with the lake," Fondzenyuy pointed at Lake Nyos.

Joseph dropped the wooden pole, placed his hands on his hips and bellowed, "What's wrong with our lake?"

"That's the world's deadliest lake," François informed him. "There are three hundred million cubic metres of lethal carbon dioxide gas at its bed. Another outgassing may occur at any time, suffocating animal life just like it did back in 1986—especially if we don't degas it quickly. Even as we're standing here, we're all at risk."

"The northern wall of Lake Nyos is greatly weakened. If it gives way, about half of the lake's water will flow through this village and three others all the way to the Nigerian border. It will trigger another disaster, far worse than what happened in the past," Murphy added, pointing towards the northern end of the lake's circular maar.

"I don't understand that your big book," Joseph retorted. "There is nothing wrong with our lake. We have performed a sacrifice to appease our gods and the spirit woman who lives in it. Nothing is going to happen there again," he told them.

"Why do you think your government razed all the villages surrounding it when the disaster happened?" François asked.

"Probably to enable you to keep testing the bomb you threw there," one of the builders said. François gasped out loud.

"That's ridiculous. Nobody tested a bomb in your lake." Murphy shook his head and started scribbling in his notebook.

"Then what caused the disaster?" the builder asked.

"The lake exploded due to intense pressure, releasing carbon dioxide gas which suffocated people," François repeated. Joseph shook his head.

"Tsiup! More big book I don't understand. I was right here in Nyos when it happened, all those years ago, it wasn't any explosion." Everybody turned in his direction. Joseph continued speaking, lowering his voice to a moody baritone.

"There is a spirit woman who inhabits Lake Nyos. That night the lake was bubbling. It sounded like the woman's grumbling. My grandfather told me she was very angry. After some time, the bubbling stopped and then she violently emerged from the lake and killed everybody around it."

François shook his head and mumbled to himself, "Ignorant fool," before asking aloud sarcastically,

"Why did she get angry and kill everybody?" The other academics laughed.

"That's because the gods of the lake were angry with us," Joseph answered, fixing his gaze on Lake Nyos, ignoring their derision.

"That is sheer legend! It's not what happened," Murphy mumbled over his notebook.

"Do you think you know what happened?" Joseph scowled.

"Yes. We didn't know before but after a thorough investigation, we do now," François answered.

"When you weren't here that night?" Joseph said, widening his eyes.

"Le fait que nous ayons été là ou pas n'a aucune importance dans nos recherches," François snapped. He began walking towards Murphy, thinking of the best way to convince Joseph who was of protozoan intellect. He signalled his other colleagues towards him, so they could discuss how to deal with his science denial.

Joseph glared at the retreating white man who hadn't witnessed that strange disaster yet claimed to know what happened. It was absurd. He laughed at the man, walked past the other builders and sat near a pole thinking, "How can he know when I was there? How can I forget the night of August 21, 1986?"

B

He was fast asleep on a mat while his grandfather was nodding on his chair when the old man started hearing a strange rumbling. He woke up and peered through the window into the clear moonlit night. The strange rumbling ceased for a couple of seconds and started again, waking Joseph. He looked around then glanced out of the window as well.

"What was that?" Joseph asked.

"I don't know," his grandfather answered.

The old man yawned and stroked his beard. Joseph walked past the lit oil lamp to the open window. He peered through it and then went to the door, which he opened, to find out where the noise was coming from. His grandfather rose from his chair and limped past his wife and great granddaughter, who were both sleeping on a small bed. He met Joseph at the door.

"Where is that sound coming from?" Joseph asked, scanning the horizon.

His grandfather didn't respond. They both stared at the grass fields, at the silhouettes of trees on the tall hills spanning the banks of Lake Nyos. Joseph saw an unusual misty cloud mushrooming above its surface.

"It is probably coming from the lake," he suggested. "I'm wondering why there is that strange mist."

"It's a sign," his grandfather said.

"What sign?"

"That sounds like grumbling to me. There is a spirit woman who inhabits Lake Nyos and other lakes in this region. I think she is angry."

Joseph continued listening. The boiling sound ceased and there was silence, except for the breathing sounds of his grandmother and niece. Joseph waited. He turned to go when suddenly: Booooom! An explosion thundered through the night air. Joseph spun around, just in time to see the lake spewing a gigantic frothy spray, which shot up hundreds of metres of vigorously effervescing gases. They were both shoved to the ground from the shock. A huge water current spawned a tsunami-like wave which surged and scoured the shore of the northern wall, shattering trees.

His grandmother and niece promptly woke up and ran to the door to see what had happened. They only saw a white gas haze over the lake rippling with floating branches. They didn't see a gas cloud spilling over the northern lip of the lake and sinking into the valley, totally hugging the ground along its path to Nyos; fast and furiously. Joseph's grandmother and niece both inhaled a pungent smell like that of rotten eggs. And after barely a few breaths, they couldn't even open their mouths because the stench had become unbearable.

Joseph's grandmother tumbled by the door and lost consciousness. His niece started fanning her nostrils with her hands. Joseph got back to his feet and pulled his niece by the collar of her blouse away from the door. He shut it tight. They both panted as he placed her back on the bed and closed the window. The little girl struggled to breath and held her chest. Joseph wanted to tell her to calm down, but no sound came from his mouth. Instead, he coughed, took a few steps forward to check on his grandparents and fell. He passed out as a strange type of warmth swept into the house.

A ray of light shone on Joseph's face. He woke with a start. Sharp needle like pains ripped through his eyes and nostrils. His ears hurt. He felt weak and nauseated. He ran his hands over his shorts and noticed honey-coloured stains patterned it. He also saw a starchy mess on his body. There were small wounds on his arms. He heard his grandfather snoring rather abnormally. The atmosphere seemed unusually devoid of all animal sounds. The flame in the oil lamp had flickered out.

He dangled towards his grandfather, shaking him. The old man moaned and tilted his head to the right. Sticky red liquids and lesions covered his wrinkled body. Joseph tried to talk to him but he couldn't. He coughed, wiped his eyes with his fingers and walked over to his grandmother. He shook her but she didn't wake up. His niece wasn't breathing either. Joseph collapsed on her lifeless little body and wept.

He woke up, swayed to the door, unbolted it and halted. He did not push it open. He stooped and then sat on the bare earth for a long time, as he struggled to breathe. When his grandfather rolled over, it occurred to him that sitting there made no sense at all. They both needed help.

What if he also died in his sleep? He was nevertheless terrified by what lay beyond the walls of their house.

He tied his handkerchief around part of his face, covering his nose, then partially opened the door. The afternoon sun seethed its incandescence on the plain, scorching the grass. He walked out after he observed that the misty cloud had cleared. He removed the handkerchief from his nose. He didn't get the rotten egg smell when he inhaled anymore. The lake looked shallower. Tree branches floated on it. Its surface had a very unattractive rusty colour, which contrasted how it looked the previous day, when it was a scenic lake, with its blue hue glistening in the sun's rays against the navy-blue skies.

He inspected the piggery and the goat house: every single livestock was dead. He decided to check on their neighbour, Ngwa. Nobody responded to his knock, so he pushed open their door and peeped. Ngwa, his wife, his grandmother and seven children all lay lifeless on different grass mattresses. A slimy liquid was smeared on their corpses which were covered in copious wounds, as if they had been trapped under a hailstone of fire. Joseph ran away, glancing at their wide-open window.

He decided to leave Nyos for Wum, a nearby village. He pushed out his motorcycle then went back and shook his grandfather. He woke up, looking frail and groggy.

"Where... is...?" his grandfather stopped in mid-sentence. Joseph knew he couldn't talk well too. He slowly pointed in the direction of his grandmother and niece. The old man turned and crept towards his wife. He buried his head on her corpse and sobbed.

Joseph patted his grandfather's shoulder and pointed at the motorcycle. The weeping old man didn't move. Joseph held him by the waist and pulled him out. They both mounted the motorcycle and took off. The thought that they were leaving behind the corpses of their loved ones haunted them both. But they had to leave. What if a second explosion occurred? Joseph rode off casting long glances at the lake. His grandfather muttered in his throat,

"Bad... lake!"

Joseph remembered what his grandfather said, that the spirit woman in Lake Nyos was angry. He knew that the villagers believed it attracted evil, so they had nicknamed it bad lake. Its reputation stemmed from Nyos folklore which told of evil spirits that had once emerged from the bottom and killed everybody in its vicinity.

Joseph pondered why the spirit woman had become angry, as he rode past herds of dead cattle. He would ask his grandfather later. He caught sight of three gory corpses straight ahead. The old man gasped, and Joseph looked away but his eyes fell on two other dead bodies on the left turn of the road. He quickly wheeled the bike around them just in time. However, the motorcycle collided with the mortal remains of a muscular man on the right turn of the road and was thrust forward in the air. Joseph and his grandfather crashed into wet elephant grass. The bike bounced off and landed elsewhere.

They lay there, their weak screams barely sounding as moans, while the motorbike's engine continued running. When they finally sat up, they were stunned by the sored cadavers of about eleven men. A putrid odour reeked from the dead bodies and punctured their nostrils, such that they felt they were inhaling and exhaling death. Joseph crawled to the motorcycle and switched it off. His grandfather whimpered and cemetery silence filled the air.

A hunter from Wum called Galega rode his bicycle from Wum towards Nyos whistling a melodious tune. The plants looked a lot greener that day. He had set up four animal traps the previous night in Nyos and was going to check on them. "What if I catch a cane rat today," he thought, ignoring the dead dove on his path. He rode on until he saw the carcass of a porcupine and halted. He picked it up and put it in his bag. He resumed his journey, until he came across the carcass of an antelope. He examined it. "This is odd," he thought. "Three different dead animals, almost in the same place." He wondered if they had all been killed by lightning. It also occurred to him that he had not ridden past anybody as he continued cycling, until he came upon a dozen dead cows.

"What is happening here?" he exclaimed in a low tone. He rode past a motorcycle that lay on the ground. When he reached a group of huts, he decided to check on its occupants. As he approached, his probing gaze was swamped by the disgusting presence of mortal remains strewn across a courtyard. Galega abandoned his bicycle and ran in the opposite direction where he had come from. He heard one of the corpses near the stalks of elephant grass cough, as he sprinted pass the motorcycle. Galega looked around fearfully and screamed. The cadaver raised its hand and spoke slowly.

"Help!"

Galega halted, focused on where the sound was coming from and returned slowly, aiming at the body he couldn't quite see in the elephant grass with his rifle. Joseph raised his head higher and their eyes met.

"What are you doing here?" Galega asked.

Joseph didn't answer. Galega saw the suppurating wounds on his body.

"I'm sorry," he stooped, examining Joseph. "What happened? There are corpses everywhere."

"We... bad air!" Joseph said.

"What does that mean?" Galega asked.

"Bad... air!" Joseph answered, pointing at his nose. His grandfather coughed. The hunter skipped away again.

"Sorry... my grandfather," Joseph pointed out in a murmur.

"Can't you talk well?"

Joseph shook his head. His grandfather sat up, blinking.

"What happened to these people?" Mr. Galega tried to find out.

"I don't... know," Joseph said.

"What do you mean you don't know?"

"Dead... fleeing... village!" Joseph's words now flowed in fragmented manner.

"And the two of you survived?"

"Yes!" they both murmured.

"Survived from what?"

"Spirit woman... struck... Nyos...," Joseph's grandfather said. He went into another coughing fit. Galega helped them up and rode them to Wum on the motorcycle for treatment.

Wum soon filled up with survivors, who stumbled in with tales of an explosion and strange smells before they'd passed out, only to wake up and discover that almost everyone around them was dead. The spirit woman story spread through Wum like cancerous cells. However, other villagers believed it had been a bomb. Local officials called the governor in Bamenda town to report the strange occurrence. The governor sent rescue teams wearing gas masks and carrying cylinders of oxygen to the affected villages.

Local and international media covered the disaster extensively. The *Herald* newspaper reported that 3,500 livestock had perished and estimated the death toll at 1,746 people. It also indicated that many of the dead had already been buried in mass graves by some survivors. The *Bamenda Post News* estimated that 4,000 people had survived but had developed serious respiratory and skin problems. It also specified that a good number of them had already fled their corpse-filled villages. Some terrified ones were taking refuge in the forest. Immediate aid was needed. The BBC reported that hundreds had been gassed in a disaster after a cloud of lethal carbon dioxide escaped from a volcanic lake in Cameroon. Government officials said on national radio that the most likely cause was a volcanic eruption which leaked gas into the atmosphere. But *The Science Observer* said this was unlikely, as the volcano was believed to be extinct. The Guinness Book of Records dubbed Lake Nyos the world's deadliest lake.

Shortly after they arrived in Wum, Joseph's grandfather got worse. Joseph sat by his sickbed. His grandfather opened his mouth, but words didn't come out. He shut his lips and smiled. He raised his feeble hands and Joseph bowed. He held Joseph's head and caressed it. The old man tilted his face and stared at Galega before turning back to Joseph. Then his frail hands slowly fell, and the old man breathed his last breath.

"He didn't tell me any more about the spirit woman. He couldn't even utter his last blessings," Joseph sobbed. Galega put his right arm around Joseph,

"Take heart my friend."

"This is too much," Joseph lamented.

"Weeh! Ashia. I'll take you to see Tergum."

"Tergum?" Joseph repeated.

"She's our most powerful soothsayer."

"Okay."

Galega led Joseph to the medicine woman's shrine. Tergum the soothsayer wore a sackcloth gown and hung a raffia bag on her left shoulder. "Come in," she ordered. "But walk backwards." The men obeyed.

"Turn around and sit." The shrine looked feral. Joseph saw skulls of dead animals and red pieces of cloth hung all over the thatch walls. He smelled numerous herbal concoctions in clay pots. Tergum gawked at Joseph, made incantatory throaty sounds and rubbed her palms. She flung something into a small pot and looked inside, then shook her head.

"When a tree produces seeds, they fall and grow around it. The Iroko tree of Nyos bore a special seed. But instead of falling and growing, it developed wings and flew away."

"Tergum, please I don't understand," Joseph confessed.

"Your chief, where is he?" Tergum asked.

"He… we don't have one. When our chief disappeared, his son who was supposed to return as his chop chair denounced the throne and went to white man country to learn big book. So, his brother became our chief instead."

"Your chief did not only abandon his throne, he also failed to lead the people in the annual sacrifice for the gods of the lakes. So, they got angry and punished Nyos and the other villages that didn't. You people will suffer until the day you do what the gods want!" Tergum prophesied. Then she untethered the two goats that Joseph had bought for her and went away. He felt disappointed that he couldn't bring back their chief.

Joseph relocated to one of the camps the government had built. Most of his immediate family and tribespeople had died. All his livestock had perished. His farms were still intact, but he couldn't go back to work there because the place had been razed and access was restricted. Earning a living became increasingly difficult, if not impossible. He suffered from serious respiratory and skin diseases. Instead of spending time on his farms, he spent it in hospitals treating his ailments. He lived in the camp unhappily, waiting for food and medication by relief agencies. He hated that he had become a permanent recipient of aid from charities. And as if that wasn't bad enough, he noticed that their aid packages kept diminishing as time passed. He even heard reports that some government officials were stealing part of it.

Tergum's words kept ringing in his head, "you people will suffer until the day you do what the gods want."

Disappointed, he decided to return to Wum and consult Tergum to ask her what the gods really wanted.

"Bring back your chief and convince him to lead the Nyos survivors to the annual sacrifice to appease the gods of the lakes," she had said.

"But he is in white man country," Joseph protested.

"He is back. He lives in Yaoundé. Find him."

Joseph organized a small delegation and they travelled to Yaoundé to look for their chief. They investigated thoroughly until they found him. They explained all what had happened and convinced him to return for his coronation and the sacrifice. His custodian brother had died in the disaster, so the prince accepted their request and returned. He was enthroned in the abandoned palace of Nyos, and finally led his people to the lake for the sacrifice of the gods.

Later, on the coronation night, several scientists drove to the lake with equipment to set up the degassing system. The next day, some Nyos survivors started returning to their ancestral land. The men built new wooden houses while the scientists assembled their lake degassing system. When the scientists learned of the resettlement, they advised the people not to return to their homes, explaining the dangers posed by Lake Nyos. But it all seemed to have fallen on deaf ears.

ℬ

After talking the issue over, the scientists went towards Joseph's team. François spoke first.

"Guys, you have to return to the camps, please. It's for your own safety."

"No way," Joseph snapped.

"Joseph, we've pleaded for too long. If you don't leave now, we'll go the hard way. We shall inform the government to evict you," Fondzenyuy warned.

"Shut up! You think I'm scared of Goment? They treated us like faeces. Inform them!" Joseph screamed.

"Young man, don't tell me to shut up," Fondzenyuy pointed his forefinger at Joseph's forehead, who pushed it away.

"I said shut up, foolish man. How can you tell your own tribesmen to abandon our village and resettle in a place of suffering when you live comfortably in town? Huh?"

Fondzenyuy slapped Joseph's right cheek. Joseph punched Fondzenyuy's face and kicked him. Joseph's friends charged at Fondzenyuy, who fell to the ground and covered his head with his hands. Nkwain went down on his knees, pleading, but Joseph's friends shoved him away. Murphy and François started a quick backward retreat in order to keep away from the impending attack. Suddenly, they both felt a sharp gust of wind coming from behind them, raising a throng of green leaves from the lake into the air. They turned around and looked. Numerous misty, human-like figures were hovering above the surface of the foggy lake.

One of the foggy beings, a gigantic one, began to rise, levitating towards them slowly. She glided over the whistling leaves as if floating on a flying mat. The men all stood stone-still, rooted to the spot in disbelief. Their hair stood on ends. Their bodies developed goosebumps. They stared at the soaring woman's glittery garments and her enigmatic beautiful face, as she loomed over them like a genie. All the villagers knelt down and bowed, including Nkwain. They all started mouthing incantations. François and Murphy watched the mystical creature, their mouths agape, wondering if what they were seeing was real. Fondzenyuy sat up and got to his knees too when she levitated towards him, although he didn't join the men to recite incantations for her. He only stared in bewilderment, sweating profusely.

Fondzenyuy felt a pang of shame for telling his own tribesmen and women to relocate to the camps. But Nyos was a high-risk zone. He believed his people had been trapped between the devil and the deep-blue sea. François glanced at Fondzenyuy, thinking: "Was the blurry image I saw on the lake just before the degassing that of this spirit woman? Was she the one Joseph had been talking about?" Murphy mused that maybe it had not been right for them to ridicule the villagers' beliefs about Lake Nyos, although he strongly felt their gas theory was correct.

The misty creature started to recoil and retreat, vanishing slowly amidst the foggy beings. The degassing system suddenly released a strong water jet into the air when she floated pass it, with nobody running its machinery.

MIAKMIAK

Momo Bertrand

Simo's palms were filled with fresh seeds. She leapt down the baobab tree and landed on the dusty red earth. She wasn't hungry, but a voice whispered to her. Reluctantly, she selected a large baobab seed from the lot she'd gathered and swallowed it without chewing. She kept the rest in her tattered brown sack. The next minute her shepherd's crook was hitting against a zebu's thin hide, and off she went, heading towards Kolofata's oasis.

The dry season was at its climax and the Sahel's sun was angry enough to keep even the most tenacious men in the shelter of their huts. But Simo was more obstinate than most men. She was considered a rebel because she found rules boring and thought their traditional practices were bizarre. Many in the village considered her weird; she was six feet tall and had a muscular body, flat chest, and a deep grave voice. Simo's character and morphology puzzled everyone in Kolofata, especially her fellow women. They didn't understand why she was so unfeminine. According to them, she was feral and uncouth, too strange by the local Hausa and Muslim standards.

When the twelve zebus reached the water point, they lined up in a queue and proceeded to drink in order of their ages. Simo raised her long, green gandora to her knees and dipped her dark feet into the clear oasis waters. She took out four tiny baobab seeds from her sack and began eating them slowly. Her hands were unclean, but she didn't care. She usually ate with unclean hands.

A light breeze blew from the east, carrying few grains of silt into her nostrils. She sneezed, scaring the zebus in the process, and laughed. It was only in moments like these that

Simo was herself. Far from home, off, rearing her father's cattle and moving through slopes, valleys, plains and hills. Out there, a few miles south of the arid Sahara Desert, dreams of cooler days dominated her psyche. She imagined herself eloping to the south with her soulmate. Migrating to that land where her strangeness would be sane.

"There, it would be normal for girls to climb trees, walk miles in the wild and rear twelve cattle; there, there would be no gender discrimination; there, most women do 'men things.' There, we would be free. I long to go there," she said, speaking to her deformed reflection on the surface of the water.

When the animals had filled their guts, Simo stepped out of the water. She quickly wiped her tears so no one would witness her cry. Her legs were still wet. Grains of white sand stuck to her soles as she journeyed homewards. Kolofata village was an hour away from the oasis, a baby's walk by Simo's standards.

ℬ

She found Papa Issa in front of the main hut. As usual, he was drunk. Comfortably seated on a purple throne-like armchair, he looked like a chief—a chief of alcohol. Before him were his servants—or masters—calabashes upon calabashes of palm wine. He was joyously singing Shakira's 'Waka Waka,' but his voice was so cranky that the song sounded more like the original Cameroonian 'Waka Waka' by the Zangalewa band.

"Daddy, what's this? Wehkeh! Why do you always disgrace us like this? Can't you get drinks and get drunk in your private hut like a civilized man?" Simo said, snatching the horn of palm wine from her father's hands.

"Disgrace? You want us to talk about disgrace?" Papa Issa screamed with closed eyes.

"Stop, daddy, not today!"

"I won't stop. Ekieh. Let's talk about dis-i-gra-ce." He spat on the ground and continued, "Look at you, my only surviving daughter. My only child. Look at you! Twenty-five years old and still you run behind cattle like a mad German Shepherd."

"Daddy, I've already told you, nature is my passion. I travel because…"

"Shut up! What kind of passion? Idiot. I brought many men to marry you and you turned them down. Even that, e-h-h, yes, that prince from Maroua wanted to pay your bride price. He wanted you just as second wife, but you refused. Your mother was my seventh wife, yet she was happy," he paused and pursed his lips. "It is unfortunate that those terrorists slaughtered my eight wives and their children that night. Un-for-tu-nate! I don't know why they spared you. They should have slaughtered you too."

He seized the horn of wine from Simo's trembling hands and added, "Next time you want to talk about disgrace, go look at a mirror, ngenom!"

A crystalline tear escaped from Simo's left eye as she ran towards her mud hut. She threw her body on the dusty floor mat and wept. She did so silently, not wanting the neighbours to think she was fragile. Everyone knew her as strong Simo. "I will run away," she said between sobs, "I will leave this ungrateful man alone."

The savoury smell of okra soup and the rhythmic sound of corn fufu being pounded in a neighbouring hut aroused her appetite. Maybe it was her imagination. Whatsoever the case, she was too proud to go ask for food from neighbours, even though okra soup was her favourite dish. That night, she slept with an empty stomach. A cold wind from the south kept her company.

When the sun took over from the moon, Simo rushed to the kraal. One by one, she freed her father's twelve zebus. One could clearly perceive ecstasy on her broad face. She felt happy because it was *MiakMiak* day and wondered why she gave such an odd and ugly name, '*MiakMiak*,' to the day she usually met her lover.

On *MiakMiak* day, Simo would be quite indulgent with the zebus. She wouldn't use her crook. Instead, she would talk to them calmly, as if they were human. "Zebu John, walk a little faster. Zebu Leonard, don't eat those poisonous herbs. Zebu Issa and Zebu Myriam, no sex in public!" The twelve zebus knew her voice and heeded to her orders.

The *MiakMiak* meeting point was at the foot of the Kapsiki hills, which was two hours away from Kolofata. When she got there, the sun had hidden behind thick nimbus clouds. Yellow elephant grass was bending slightly eastwards under the weight of the Harmattan winds. The mixed smell of fresh dung and fresh grass filled the air. Simo lay on the turf and waited. The twelve zebus strayed about, grazing.

After about an hour, a black spot appeared on the horizon. The spot became a patch, which grew into a large herd of cattle. At its rear was a short, light-skinned woman. Her huge pointed breasts pushed against a dazzling red gandora.

Simo rushed towards the short woman. They hugged each other tightly amidst tears of joy. When they kissed, the cattle from both herds mooed. When the touching was over, Amina whispered into Simo's ear, "I love you, my sweet yam."

"I love you too, Amina. We will run away soon, to a land where our love won't be a crime."

"In the south, people don't care. Not like the bigots we have here, idiotic like Zebu Leonard," Simo said.

While they ate yellow yams and okra soup which Amina had brought, they spoke about their escape. Their plan was simple. On the first day of the Ramadan month, they would each sell five of their fathers' zebus, then walk to Maroua. There, they would use the cash from the cattle sales to hire a car that would take them far away, south-bound. Once they were far enough, they would rent a small room, start a trade and live happily ever after. However, Ramadan was still nine months away, and all they had for now was this lofty dream and *MiakMiak* day once every week.

"I love you, Amina. Promise me we'll always be together."

"I promise you, Simo, I promise," Amina replied, kissing Simo's shoulder.

By the time the two lovers parted, stars had already taken over the sky. They shone a little brighter than the moon. Only the sound of mating crickets broke the cold silence of the Sahel night. Simo walked hastily towards the village because the cattle detested staying out late, and she was scared of djinns, malevolent spirits who inhabit the earth and assume various forms. As she hurried home, several thoughts stormed her mind: Amina's soft red lips, Zebu Leonard's stubbornness, her escape, and serenity.

ℬ

Everywhere was silent when Simo returned. She quickly led the zebus to the kraal and checked the main hut, which was empty. Daddy must be out drinking, she thought, as she got into her tiny hut and slept almost immediately.

In the middle of the night, she was awakened by a strident cry. It seemed to come from the direction of the market square. "Where is this noise coming from?" she thought, as her heart raced. She got dressed picked her brown bag and went towards her dad's hut. It was still empty. After a brief hesitation, she resolved to get to the market, where the sound seemed to be coming from. The lunar light was just bright enough to enable her run at a steady pace without tumbling over a rock. The cries grew louder as she got closer. Intermittently, she could hear the sound of metal hitting against metal.

When she was a few yards from the square, she slowed down her steps and crouched. She tried unsuccessfully to slow down her breathing as she crept slowly in a dusty alley between a soya store and a tailor's workshop. She stopped. Lying there, she could see all the villagers. She counted about 65 of them, seated in a wide circle in the market's central space. Men and women, young and old, as well as toddlers. All were silent. A huge fire in the middle of the circle made the dread on their faces clearly distinguishable. She spotted her father, seated with a stoic face between two younger women. Standing behind the villagers were about 50 men dressed in black military uniforms. They held bloody swords in both hands.

She also noticed that the strange sound came from eight newborn babies who lay between the villagers and the fire. Their arms and legs had been cut off. Blood oozed out from their amputated limbs. Limb-like shapes were burning in the huge fire in the middle of the circle, and there was a smell like that of roasted pork in the air.

One of the men in a black military uniform shouted in Hausa, "You people have defied Islam. You have let the infidels come and settle amongst you. You all merit death. We have slain and burnt the bastard children you gave birth to. Now, in the name of Allah, we will kill all of you."

Suddenly, the 50 men shouted, "Long live Boko Haram!" and in a quick and precise manner, they slit the villagers' throats. Simo watched the terrorists kill her father and 64 other villagers but couldn't do anything to stop them from committing this atrocity. The feeling of powerlessness that overcame her caused warm tears to trickle from her eyes, as she wailed.

She didn't realize her wailing had been heard by the terrorists until one of them shouted, "There's someone there in the dark!" Upon hearing this, Simo sprang up like a Goliath frog and ran away. When she was certain no one was chasing her, she slowed down her pace. She'd been running for about two hours.

When she finally stopped, she felt a sharp pain in her chest. She lay under a date tree and gazed at the sky. After about an hour of silence, she wept, "I know You expect me to thank You for saving my life. But first, I have a question. Why? Allah, why? Why did You let this happen? Couldn't You save just the babies?" There was silence. She tried to cry, but her tear glands were dry.

She could not return to her village. Everybody there was probably dead by now. "Allah, I asked You to help me escape. I didn't ask You to kill everyone I would leave behind. Is this the plan You had for me?" She scratched her left ear and then spoke out loudly, "I hope You kept Amina safe. I will go get her and we will run away."

When day broke, she went off towards Amina's village. From a distance, her eyes beheld a dreadful sight. Huge red flames and dark smoke emanated from her lover's village. Her worst fear had been confirmed: Boko Haram had raided Amina's village.

"They killed her! I have no reason to live anymore," Simo said, as she fell on her knees and picked up a sharp stone, determined to take away her life. But before she could cut her veins, she heard a soft voice which told her to follow her dream and go south, towards her freedom.

After a brief hesitation, she began journeying southwards. At the Kolofata oasis, she drank as much as her guts could hold. She then walked further south, past the

Kapsiki hills where the *MiakMiak* rendezvous usually took place.

"I will follow this road and reach Maroua by evening. Surely, a bus driver will be kind enough to take me to Freedom City for free," she thought. Simo was right on the first point: she reached Maroua's bus park by dusk. However, none of the bus drivers agreed to take her south for free. Instead, they made derogatory statements: "You think it's your father's car, fool!" "You have more muscles than my son, just start running. You will surely reach before Ramadan." One even asked her to sleep with him for the lift.

Trekking was the only option left because she had no friends in Maroua and she couldn't return to her village. She longed to be free, to reach Freedom City, where all things would be possible. "Surely, the southerners would be friendlier. They will give me food, shelter and maybe a few cattle," she thought. "Trek, I must."

So she continued her journey southwards, walking on the thin winding road that led to Freedom City. She strode mostly by night and rested during the day to avoid the scorch of the Sahel sun. When her baobab seeds were exhausted, she survived on wild herbs, bitter fruits and crickets. She drank water from clear springs, shallow streams and even muddy ponds. Sometimes, bus drivers would pass and notice her. Like the priest in the parable of the Good Samaritan, they would speed off, shaking the dust off their buses' tyres as they went. Simo didn't care. She kept walking.

On the seventh day of her voyage, she leaned against the trunk of a tree on the side of a footpath. She was thirsty. She had seen no water point for miles, and she was dehydrated. She longed to squeeze water out of the flies that buzzed about her head, but she was too exhausted to do so. She closed her eyes and rested, hoping to open them amidst a choir of alhamdulillah-singing angels.

They were not exactly angels. Yet, the five UN blue berets seemed to be sent by Allah. One of them noticed Simo's immobile body while he relieved himself. "There's a girl over here. She's alive!" he screamed. He called on the others to move her to their sky-blue jeep. There, a doctor gave her a glucose drip.

Simo woke up six hours later. It was midnight. She was lying on a blanket in a thorny bush. There were five men a few metres away from her. Seeing them, she was surprised but her face didn't show it. The five soldiers were seated around a fire, arguing loudly. She caught glimpses of what they said. "She is awake…" "… do it now… easy." "Will it be okay… for real?" "I will start…" "OK guys… let's do it!"

Suddenly, four men were holding her to the ground. One man was between her lower limbs, making quick to and fro movements. She was barely awake. When he finished, he in turn went and held a limb and another came and replaced him between her thighs. The cycle continued until five nations violated her. When they had finished, they went back and sat around the fire, jubilantly commenting on the speed, vigour and style of each man. They joked about the whole thing.

Simo lay silent. The pain between her legs was unbearable and she couldn't forget the sight of the soldiers taking turns to make her suffer.

Looking up, Simo could see the full moon. It glowed like the sun. She wished she could go there, to the moon. She would live there with Amina. On the moon, there would be no beasts in blue berets. No drunken fathers. No impious bus drivers. It was in the midst of this contemplation that she lost consciousness.

ℬ

When she woke up, the moon had hidden behind the horizon. She was lying on a thick spring bed in a well-lit room with white walls. There was a pungent smell of disinfectant in the air. 'We are the World' was playing from a loudspeaker on the ceiling. She also noticed that her garments had been changed. Her pale yellow gown was gone. She now wore a light-pink garment on which it was written CENTRAL HOSPITAL, FREEDOM CITY in red ink.

The five UN soldiers were seated on purple armchairs beside the door and chatting. As soon as they noticed that Simo's eyes were open, they stopped. One of them dashed out of the ward. He returned minutes later with eight journalists. The four remaining soldiers stood up and came close to Simo's bed as the journalists and fifth soldier approached the bed.

"What happened?" a journalist from Africa24 asked.

The five men looked at each other. After about thirty seconds of muteness, one of them cleared his throat and spoke, "We were patrolling the area around Maroua two days ago when we fell on a group of Boko Haram terrorists. We noticed they were trying to rape this poor girl. Luckily, they didn't hear us coming, so we engaged fire and killed them all, ehh… five men in total."

He paused, looked at his comrades and took a dramatic tone, "Unfortunately, we realized they had already assaulted her, so we took her to our vehicle and drove as fast as we could till we reached Freedom City's Central Hospital yesterday night. She received intensive care. We all decided to stay here till she recovered fully."

As if a signal had been given, tears escaped the soldiers' eyes almost simultaneously. "We are not heroes. The true hero is her," the soldier who was narrating the story concluded. The journalists clapped for the five men. After asking for the soldiers' names and taking pictures, they went off, eager to publish the story. No one cared about Simo's version. She watched the whole scene in dismay. Her guts were filled with a cocktail of bitter emotions, and she was disgusted by the soldiers.

She stood up and walked to the window. Looking down, her sight fell on a sea of gorgeous people with colourful dresses as they walked graciously up and down the marble pavements. They looked lovely and welcoming. This vision matched the expectations which Simo had about Freedom City. This gave her hope. "Surely, there is a soulmate waiting for me down there," she thought. "Perhaps Amina somehow survived. If that were the case,

I'll find her and we will have *MiakMiak* days till the end of time. I will be free... I am free."

MY SUICIDE EXPLAINED

Rita Bakop

Translated from the French by Emma Fredgant

I know this will hurt, Mom. Right now I'm on the roof of the Hilton Hotel, and I'm going to jump. By the time you get this letter, I'll be dead, but if you read until the end, you'll know what pushed me to do this. Please read carefully.

It all started on the day I had to go dancing at Java Night Club with my friends Ateba and Awalou. I know you don't like them because you always thought that they were too young for all the bad things they knew and did. I don't know why you said that: probably your maternal instinct. Maybe you were right... I asked you for permission and you refused, do you remember? I've always been stubborn, so I scaled the fence while you were sleeping. I was so proud of myself, you know! Awalou and Ateba waited for me in a car, not far from the house.

When we got to the club, it was a dream! Mom, I had only ever seen things like that on television! For a seventeen-year-old whose hormones are still raging, it was ecstasy. We danced for hours and then I went to sit down because I was starting to feel tired. That's when I noticed this very pretty girl casting furtive glances at me. She had glowing dark skin, with long, curly hair, the ends of which she had woven into a pretty braid that fell onto her left shoulder. She was about 1.6 m tall and her gestures bespoke sophistication. I walked over to her and introduced myself.

"Hello, I'm Jeff Yalla. And you are...?"

"I'm Leila," she replied.

"How about grabbing a drink together?"

"What a polite young man! Enough with the formality, Jeff."

"Alright, Leila. So let's sit, and then we can have that drink?" I said, putting in all my charm.

"Whatever you want, I'm here to have fun anyway."

After a few sips of a martini–yes, Mom, you always thought that I didn't drink alcohol, but that day I drank some–Ateba and Awalou came to sit with us. That's when the surprises started.

"You see the gift we gave you?" Ateba asked me, with a half smile.

"What gift, where is it?" I replied, quite confused.

"Leila, obviously! She's your present," Ateba laughed. "You really think a bombshell like her would have agreed to talk to a guy like you over a martini without a good reason?"

"Oh! Well… thanks. Great present!" I said, even more confused.

"What's more, we're going to make you just as rich as we are. You'll see," Awalou chimed in very confidently.

"Yeah, that's why I'm staying here with you. Come on, we're going to introduce you to some people," Leila, who had been observing us without saying a word, added.

They took me to a corner of the club where four men in black suits and blue shirts were seated. I started to feel frightened. This all seemed so shifty. One of the men, probably the ringleader, started talking. He told me to relax–they weren't going to eat me. Straight away, he continued on to say that this was a group of paederasts. He told me just like that, Mom, in no veiled terms. I was horrified. That's when my friends told me that they had also been roped into this "association," just like me, and that it was where their money came from.

I stood up and headed for the exit, thinking I could just leave. One of the men advised me to stay where I was, but I didn't listen, despite his dark looks and the air of excessive confidence that he gave off. When I reached the door, the bouncer stopped me and calmly asked for the password.

"What password? So one now needs a password to leave a nightclub?" I shouted in anger. I just wanted to be gone from there.

"No, but when you chat with the G4, you need a password to leave. So you have two options: either you give me the password and you leave, or you go back and sit down before I bash your face in."

The bouncer delivered these words so authoritatively that it made my blood curdle for a second. I turned my head slightly and saw the sardonic smiles on their faces. I went back and sat down beside them. My mind was assailed by a mixture of fear, shame, and above all, hatred for my friends. Dragon—the ringleader—took out a wad of banknotes from his pocket and made three stacks, two of 300,000 francs and another of 200,000 francs.

"Alright, Ateba, Awalou, here's the payment promised for bringing us a new member, and the security deposit guaranteeing that you will be ours again for four good months," he said, giving my friends a stack of 300,000 francs each.

"This, my girl, is for you; you'll need to spruce up your wardrobe so you can attract more guys," he continued, giving Leila the last stack. "As for you, my dear Jeff, we have to tell you that one thing we don't like at all is disrespect, and what you just did is pure contempt. You see four men dressed like us and you think that someone like you, only halfway out the birth canal, can defy us? You're foolish, kid. Truly foolish."

"You know what happens to people who act like you did? They get a special punishment. And we know all about you, you know. Your mother, suffering from tuberculosis; your father, who doesn't care about you at all; your education, about to come to an end; the misery you live in... My dear, that's a lot to deal with, don't you think?" another member of the G4 reeled off while smoking a cigar. His name was Cobra.

"How do you know all that about me?" I asked, feeling angry and disgusted, like throwing up.

"You don't ask the questions here," Cobra replied. "Let's take a little walk, Jeff Yalla."

Then one of them seized my arm and twisted it to my back, pushing me towards the exit.

"Where are you taking me? What do you want with me? Let me go!" I shouted amid the din of the nightclub and the drunk people around, as if anyone would care.

"What's wrong with you all of a sudden, kid? Don't you like walks anymore? Your file tells us it's one of your favourite pastimes. Come on, don't be shy!" the third man, the one called Python, said cynically. "Ateba and Awalou, mission accomplished. Leila, don't stay here, it's dangerous."

They took me to a house that looked abandoned, but was very well furnished. It was definitely on the outskirts of the city because there were hardly any houses nearby. As we entered the house, the fourth man–Varan, who had been silent all this time–pushed me onto a chair. His face was impassive and I asked myself what he was thinking. I thought he was a mute until the moment he rather curtly said, "Kalashnikov!" Unaware of my predicament, I thought that was the name of one of his accomplices. That's when I saw a firearm for the first time in my life, in front of my face! Then he ordered:

"Take off your pants!"

"Why?" I asked, frightened and confused, trying to gain as much time as possible.

"Don't make me do it for you!"

I did it as mechanically as possible. He ordered me to lean forward. I felt something icy on my rear: it was the cap of the Kalashnikov being slowly inserted…I can't find the strength to tell you where, but you can surely guess what they put me through.

The next day, I stayed in bed all day. You probably thought I slept for so long because I was tired from the night before. You were right, sort of. You blamed me for being disobedient and idle all day. You can't understand how much my backside ached. It was one week before the baccalaureate exams. Now you can understand why I failed. Ateba and Awalou were out of sight throughout that week.

One day, we crossed paths in a Santa Lucia supermarket. They wanted to avoid me, but they couldn't, because there wasn't much of a distance separating us.

"I thought we were friends."

"But we are!" Awalou responded.

"So why did you drag me into this?"

"It was our ticket to immunity. It was either you or death, so we saved our lives," Awalou said, avoiding eye contact with me.

"But really, what were you thinking when you tried to leave the nightclub like that? You probably got the Kalashnikov treatment!" Ateba said in turn.

"So you knew what you were getting me into! You're such hypocrites! And you told them everything about me, from my sick mother to my family's situation!"

"You can't really escape these people; they know everything they want to know. Think about your sick mother! Thanks to this, we have money to buy swanky clothes and get the hottest girls at school. Our popularity stems from our meeting the G4. You should be thanking us, not getting angry," Ateba said, almost scoldingly.

"And, to be honest, you don't really have a choice. Either you cooperate with these people, or you die. Correct me if I'm wrong, but you cherish your life, don't you?" Awalou said.

On that note, they left me standing in the perfume aisle of the supermarket. When I got back to the house, I thought about the conversation I had had with my "friends." I thought about you and all of our family's problems. I thought about how you left a man who had always denied me, who always said I wasn't his offspring. A few seconds later, I got a phone call from an anonymous number, but I recognized the voice. He said, "cooperate or die!" His tone was emphatic. That's when I decided to go stay with Grandma in the village. However, even that far away from town, I still got threats.

B

Two months later, your tuberculosis got worse. You had to stay in the local hospital. So I came back home. Considering that neither dad nor his family cared about us, and that Grandma was the only person we had in the world, we didn't have the means to pay for your full treatment. I tried to find work here and there, all in vain. Dragon called me constantly to warn me of the risk I was taking. I eventually had to join their paederastic circle, as your state was getting worse every day. They didn't subject me to the torment of the Kalashnikov anymore. It was less painful this time, even though, within me, I felt worse than ever, because I was "prostituting" myself. I had turned away from Christian morality (I know, I was never as pious as you, but at that moment I thought of God).

After they forced themselves on me, they would take out a wad of 350,000 francs and give it to me. I envisioned you, my mother, who would soon be back on her feet and I went to the hospital to pay for your medical bills.

"Where did you get all this money from, son?" you asked once.

"During the vacation, I did some odd jobs as a builder's aide, a carpenter's apprentice, and a cybercafé attendant... These different wages paid for your bills," I lied.

"Son, you didn't have to sacrifice your money for your old mom. Look at you, a teenager, full of life, a life full of promise. I have nothing left to win or to lose."

"Mom, you're the person I love most in the world. I couldn't have stood your death knowing that I could have done something to help you survive."

"Thank you, Jeff. That goes straight to my heart. You're the only man I can count on."

ℬ

This charade lasted for months, up to the day when the doctor announced that you could leave the hospital: you were finally cured. We were so happy. On the way home, we had a short conversation:

"You've been very well dressed recently, Jeff. What's going on?"

"Oh, nothing, just decided to change for a bit."

"Ah, I see. So, who's the girl that's caught my son's eye?"

I blushed and responded, looking down:

"You're psychic now?"

"No, but you are my son, sweet and full of life. When a young man starts to care about how he looks, it's because something has pushed him to it. I hope I can meet her one of these days."

I was indeed in love–I think–with a girl from my class. She was very pretty and fairly sought-after. We got along well, and she was particularly sweet with me. I would have liked to believe that she was just as enamoured of me...

After the last time they had their way with me—the time that allowed me to pay for your last bill—I didn't want to be one of the G4s' henchmen anymore, or rather I wanted to stop being one of their objects. I've always believed that life is as I imagine it; simple and without pitfalls. That's when they informed me that once you're part of G4, you're in it for life.

"What if one gets tired?"

"Tired of what, life?" Cobra asked me.

"No, tired of being dehumanized each week for 350,000 CFA francs!"

"Oh! I see! Now that his mommy is well, he's 'tired of being dehumanized for 350,000 CFA francs each week!'" he bellowed out in memorable laughter.

"We told you that once you're with us, you're with us for life. Even if you went into exile, you would always find another group of G4s. Your file is everywhere, you know!" Python added.

"Unless you decide to jump off a building," Varan, who never said more than two consecutive phrases, added cynically.

That is when the gravity of the situation dawned on me. I therefore went to see the police commissioner.

"My boy, young people like you have already been here several times, and it always ends the same way."

"What do you mean by that, sir?"

"Son, you haven't even lost all your milk teeth and you want to defy these men? Clearly you don't understand what you're dealing with! Come, let me show you something."

"What's that?" I asked.

"Come on, you'll see for yourself."

He took me into a dreary room with a small chair and light bulb letting off only a weak, sad light. I immediately recognized a torture room. I wanted to leave but two police officers caught me, seized me forcibly. The police chief gave some instructions, then the men made me sit on the chair and started to hit me all over my body. They beat me like no one ever had. They continued until I passed out. When I woke up, I was in the police station's infirmary.

When I got out, Dragon and Varan were waiting for me in front of their black vehicle. They didn't give me a chance to speak; Varan started punching me all over my face, even though I was already in bad shape. My face was bleeding. As soon as he finished hitting me, Varan said "you just signed your own death warrant," before letting me go.

At the house, I told you that I got beat up by a band of criminals because I didn't have any money on me. I know that you suspected something because of how much you asked me if everything was okay. That was three days ago.

ℬ

This morning, I went out for some exercise. I was kidnapped by the paederasts. They took me into their hotel room. They each forced themselves on me one last time, one after the other. Varan showed me once more that he had earned his brown belt in karate. Afterwards, he ordered the bouncer I met the first day to take me up to the roof and to push me off. A murder passed off as suicide! You can't believe how smart these guys are! The bouncer in question forced me to the roof of the hotel. I cried like a baby. He had a notepad and a pen, so I asked him if I could write you this letter. He agreed, and said:

"When I look at you, I see a pure soul. I'm truly sorry to see you die so young. But you know, I can't do otherwise. If I save you, I die. I'm a father of two. So once you finish writing this letter you will jump by yourself, or I'll push you off myself."

Mom, think of everything good I have done, forgive me for everything I did to you, take care of yourself and don't cry. My sweet mother, I love you with all my heart. Life is beautiful, I know, but I don't want you to blame me. Pray for my soul.

Here I go…

BLACK STAR

Dipita Kwa

For 13 months now, 14 people from nine different families had been hiding here with no hope of ever returning home. Eleven-year-old Pungu Alphonse Dikalo longed for the day he would stop sleeping on a mat in this tent built by women and children in a cocoa farm in the heart of the bush. The tent was constructed with wooden poles pinned in a rough rectangle between cocoa trees and roofed with an old tarpaulin that was once used to sun cocoa seeds. The green leaves of the cocoa trees above the tarpaulin served as camouflage against military surveillance planes. The rest of the empty walls not covered by the falling ears of the tarpaulin roof were lined with palm branches and grass.

The women cooked outside under the shade of a mango tree. The outhouse, dug by Pungu and two other younger boys, was a narrow trench of about a metre deep, a metre wide and two-and-a-half metres long. The top was crossed with wooden bars trimmed flat on the surface for users to safely step on and squat without sliding and falling into the hole. It was also walled with palm branches but had no roof, so that when it rained, water leaked from the leaves of cocoa plants unto the bare backs and buttocks of the latrine user.

Most nights Pungu dreamt of the warmth of his bed in his room back in the village. He could never get used to sleeping on a mat with three other children on a hard, rough floor. Apart from famine, they lived with the permanent danger of snakes and wild insects that could crawl in through the gaping entrance, or any of the numerous holes on the roof and walls, and swallow or bite anyone in their sleep. He wondered if there was a better way to die. Not because he wanted to die. But the choices before

Pungu aligned with the meaning of his name. With such odds at the moment, it wasn't about if you died, it was about how you died. What was the difference, dying from a soldier's bullets back in the village or dying from the poisonous bite of a green mamba in the forest? He wasn't sure even his father who abandoned him here knew the answer. Maybe he would say that the former was certain, while the latter was probable.

Every night Pungu battled with mosquitoes, rain, and cold, but above all these was the fear of a snake crawling inside his T-shirt in search of warmth and coiling with its head close to his neck.

This night was specifically horrific.

"I am dying…" came that dreadful faint cry of anguish again. In the early hours of the morning, Maura had wailed and thrashed in pain, but now she was exhausted. The words barely seeped out of her tired lips.

Pungu peeped from under the wrapper covering his body from feet to ears. He had stopped waiting anxiously to hear the sweet cry of a newborn baby and instead focused on switching his mind to a beautiful memory of a distant past when peace and merriment flourished in the land. But the force of the crisis in the room this dawn was stronger than his fertile imagination could break away from.

"Put your hands here," Big Mama Nyame instructed Timou who was sweating and trembling with fear and apprehension. Pungu couldn't blame the girl. She was only twelve. And it was her mother who was agonizing.

"Both hands!" Mama Nyame scolded. "Press hard! The baby is going up instead of going down."

Timou whimpered as she knelt on the mattress beside Maura her mother. She placed her palms below Maura's naked breasts slightly above her equally naked bulging belly. There were three other women who shared the tent with Maura, Mama Nyame, Timou and the eight children. The children addressed them as Auntie except Maura who vehemently refused this title, saying it made her feel old. Auntie Pauline was fanning the flame on the damp fireplace outside to boil a pot of water. Auntie Yaya held Maura's knees raised and pulled wide apart, while Auntie Sophie held on to Maura's thrashing arms and mopped sweat and sputum from her face with a wet piece of cloth.

Pungu listened to Auntie Yaya explain to Timou that the slimy, bloody liquid on the mattress was Maura's *water* that had burst to enable the baby to swim out. Like Timou, Pungu had never witnessed a birthing scene. He never knew that it took so much pain and time for a woman to bring forth life.

"Her time is long overdue. If it continues like this, we shall have to operate her and take out the child, otherwise both of them will die," Big Mama Nyame said, as if she was talking to herself.

Timou wailed and put both hands on her head. Six-year-old Lawar sleeping next to Pungu also began to cry. Pungu closed his ears with both hands.

"Get out, all of you," Auntie Yaya called out to the children. "Pungu, take your brothers and sisters out. Go to the stream and fish or bathe or fetch water. Go out, anywhere!"

Pungu almost smiled at the attribution of a filial link between him and the other children sharing this beggarly existence. He got up, calling out to the other children, all dressed in worn-out clothes that hung over their scaly skins like rags. They scurried out of the tent with Pungu who was relieved from having to witness how Maura's belly would be cut open. What were the women going to use? Certainly a rusty razor blade if they ever found one among their belongings in this bush house. Or they may use the sharp edge of the leaf of an elephant grass. That was what was used to tear Lawar's boil.

Pungu sent the children away to wash their faces and play. He stooped under the tree that served as a kitchen shade and watched Auntie Pauline fanning the flame under the sooty pot of water. Her eyes glistened with tears probably forced out by the smoke, or Maura's predicament, or the peppery remnants of her own crushed dreams and bleak hopes.

Like the thousands living in bushes and as refugees in neighbouring cities and countries, Pungu's life was disrupted when the peaceful protest by Anglophone civil society activists turned into an armed struggle for separation. They'd requested reforms in the educational and legal systems affecting the country's two English-speaking regions. His father, Dikalo La Ngoss'a Pungu, now lived in one of the Ambazonian militia camps where he served as a cook. Only a few stubborn old men and women stayed back in the village, preferring to wait for death in their homes rather than to live in bushes like wild animals. And death eventually met many when the villages were raided, people were gunned down, and houses burnt with old people inside.

With most men living in hiding in rebel camps under strict juju restrictions, Pungu marvelled at when and where women like Maura could meet with the men who got them pregnant. He couldn't understand how any sensible woman would decide to engage in the process of bringing forth life in such miserable conditions. Not that there was any hospital around Bonabato, even before the crisis broke out. But babies are to be born in clean hospitals where, on stepping out from their mother's womb, they are supposed to see smiling nurses in their immaculate white robes. A place where neighbours, friends and family joyfully visit the new mothers with baskets of fruits and food, and bottles of mineral water and beer. Births were joyful moments. But here in this shack built on a farm close to a swamp, several kilometres from civilization, a pregnant woman like Maura surrendered herself to nature's verdict on whether or not she and her babies would live or die in the process of procreation.

Maura had never gone for a single prenatal medical consultation because it was impossible to go back to the village. It was a suicidal move, a self-imposed death penalty by means of stray bullets from the soldiers patrolling in vehicles with the thirsty nozzles of automatic rifles and machine guns pointing out, sniffing for blood, ready to drill holes into any human being on sight.

Pungu recalled that this was the second consecutive year that they hadn't gone to school, and he wasn't sure he would ever go to school again. Their village school building, built by the contributions from their parents' farming income, was now a heap of charred bricks, wood and iron. Today he would have been in secondary school like his lucky friend Bambi whose parents had fled with him to live with his uncle in Douala immediately after the crisis had started. Bambi was now in Form One.

As he pondered his fate, an idea slowly crept into his mind. He could for once break the rules by refusing to be a coward and take a serious risk. As the oldest boy in the house, it was incumbent upon him to do something to save Maura and her baby. He could return to the village to look for a "push-truck" or a wheelbarrow in which Maura could be carried back to the village. Once in the village, with some luck, they might see a vehicle to take her to the hospital in Tiko.

Pungu nodded and smiled as he told himself that it was a brilliant idea. He sneaked away behind cocoa trees as discretely as he could. Once out of sight, he started running. He knew this forest very well. He ran non-stop, his steps made light by the purity of his intention to save lives and the craving to see his village again after such a long time away. He met nobody on the way, avoiding the open roads and keeping mostly to footpaths and under the shade of trees. From what he had heard, the soldiers had been given the mission to eradicate the entire male population of the two English-speaking regions, killing anyone who could pose a threat of resistance both in the present and in distant horizon of at least 50 years to come.

There was a chilling silence in the village when he got close. The air was still and stale as though nature was mourning the absence of human life. Pungu began to feel that his task was unachievable. He crawled behind the church building. Even the Seminarians had fled. Why wouldn't they? Nowadays, a priest gets shot to death and all the church does is fold her tail and growl in a dark corner like a scared dog. Even the church had lost its critical moral voice in the face of the evil perpetrated by a tyrannical government. Everyone was afraid to point a finger at the malice.

A few goats sat chewing the cud on the broken concrete veranda of the catechist's house. Pungu went through a space in the hedge separating the church compound from the main road, crossed the road and ran into their compound. He pulled aside a loose plank behind the back door frame, put his hand in and pulled back the iron lever, opening the door. He entered the quiet, abandoned house and went straight into his room. The window of his room opened directly to the street separating their home from the church compound so that standing behind his open window, he could see anyone who came and went. Pungu opened the window to send out the stale air and to have a quick escape route should danger come knocking on the back door.

He sat on his bed and began to plan his next move. The mouldy smell in the room made him sneeze. He satisfied his yearning desire by resting his back on his soft mattress. He closed his eyes and enjoyed this long-awaited moment. It wasn't as he'd thought. He instead felt sad. Everything that made life in Bonabato fun stood the risk of disappointing Pungu.

Beside the pillow was a cap he had fabricated back in those days when life in Bonabato was still full of fun, hope and laughter. He picked up the cap, lay flat on his back, gazed at the roof made of rusty aluminium sheets, and let his mind wander away like a bird freed from a cage. As though to bury the present pile of sadness by overlaying it with a flowery painting of what had once been the life of many now living in misery and grief in various hideouts, Pungu's mind took him to a memorable football match, one Sunday afternoon.

It was the last Sunday of August 2015, one year before the crisis began, and the rain had beaten hard on Bonabato the whole night before. Pungu slept soundly, dreaming of the final football match between the Black Stars of Bonabato and the Vultures of Bonamikenge. That afternoon, after church service ended, he locked himself in his room to fabricate his supporter's gear. The paper cap was easier to make using cardboard and an elastic band from some old underwear to hold it tight on his head. However, in order to write the name and number on his worn sky-blue T-shirt, he had to recover paint from a discarded paint bucket by pouring kerosene into it and pounding it with a piece of wood. Then he added some ink extracted from the filament of a pen and made a brush by chewing one end of a harvested piece of hibiscus stem into fine, flexible fibres. With his paint and brush ready, he cut out letters and a number in a piece of cardboard. He then spread the T-shirt on his bed, placed the cardboard on it and diligently applied the paint on the cut-out shapes using the chewing stick brush.

When he was finally done and held out the finished work to the light of the open window, he noticed that the letters were blotted on the edges. Only the number "9" stood out clearly. Had he spread the shirt on a hard, smooth surface, the BLACK STAR sign in the middle would have looked actually like a real star instead of looking like a star infected with chickenpox. He'd also made a flag with a black star in the middle using a paper cut in the form of a triangle glued against a piece of bamboo. The black star was painted with charcoal.

The sound of the whistles from the football field didn't let him wait for the paint to dry. He quickly but carefully pulled on his T-shirt and wore his cap, fastening the elastic band above his ears. He could feel the wetness of the paint on his back as the T-shirt stuck against his skin like plaster, but he didn't care. He locked the main door and ran out of the house. Pungu wanted to be among the first persons to get to the football field, but when he finally got to the school yard, he saw that half of the village had already assembled. Men, women and children crowded the four corners of the field, waiting for the players to arrive, and for the football match to start. The various lines were clearly demarcated with wood ash so that from one end of the field, one could easily spot the large circle that marked the penalty spot on the other end.

Like most Bonabatos, Pungu had grown up knowing that Sunday and Tuesday afternoons were hilarious moments for the people during the inter-quarter football tournament season which was usually organized during the long, third term holidays. Football had always been one of the most important pastimes and the unifying event in a community where everyone's mind was preoccupied by farming and fishing matters on every other day of the week. For two and a half months after schools went on vacation, men, women and children, the old and the young alike, anxiously looked forward to the Sundays and Tuesdays when the matches were played. And this particular Sunday was the most awaited.

Pungu smiled when he spotted their next-door neighbour Maura, a smallish woman in her early thirties who adored lipstick and high heel shoes to compensate for her deficient stature. She couldn't be more than a metre and sixty. This afternoon she was wearing a pair of salamander shoes with solid, thick wooden heels, and standing under the shade of her new rainbow-coloured umbrella even though there was neither sunshine nor rain. She was chewing gum and her blue lipstick shone from where she stood beside the corner-kick box.

That morning, before going to church, Pungu saw Maura put out her dress and shoes on the drying-line on her veranda. She never wore these clothes to church on Sundays because they were special attires to be worn for mass appreciation, and the football field was exactly the place to flaunt a beautiful body clad in a beautiful dress.

From Maura, Pungu let his gaze roam the grandstand where two loudspeakers were mounted and the commentator, the Class 6 teacher, was proudly repeating,

"Allo, Allo... testing... testing," into a red FM microphone.

Pungu smiled as he heard the jingle of the bell. The Black Stars had arrived! There were loud shouts and applause as soon as the crowd heard the bells. And there they were, the Black Stars of Bonabato, dressed in a new set of white jerseys. The goalkeeper was in front, leading his team with a new hurricane lamp in one hand. They walked in a single file, one player directly behind the other, holding hands in a bond of unified determination. The captain was the last behind. He carried a new football and a white plastic bag containing table salt and uncooked rice.

Pungu and his friends jumped around waving their flags as the players ran onto the pitch. The captain opened his plastic bag of rice and salt and began a running tour of the field, sprinkling the various demarcation lines with the salt and the rice, beginning from the goalpost.

A wonderful beginning of a spectacle, if not for the sudden entrance of the Vultures. Players bursting individually from various corners of the field like a flock of birds dispersed by the firing of a gun. They were dressed in red shirts over red pants. It was a sight to see. Shortly after the arrival of both teams, the referee summoned the two captains, tossed the coin to determine on which side each team would commence. Then the Vultures ran to their side of the field and formed a tight line across their goalpost from one pole to the other, arms chained around the elbows.

"They are building a mountain," someone beside Pungu said.

When the referee finally blew the kick-off whistle, another level of excitement seized the crowd. Men, women and children jeered, cheered and booed. Tension quickly mounted as the minutes progressed. With no goal from either side, anger began to flare. In his shifty excitement, Pungu found himself close to where Maura danced around, saying provocative slangs to old female rivals, most of whom backed off, ignoring her. Pungu didn't hear what Maura said to Pauline, the woman who owned a drinking spot at Four-corners. He only heard Pauline proclaim that the father of Maura's daughter Timou was a swindler.

"Jealousy is a show of mental poverty," Maura shouted, beating her lips with her palms, producing a trumpeting sound and jumping on the spot in taunting excitement. "At your age you go out with men old enough to be your grandfather. Are you not ashamed?"

"It is better than using charms to steal people's husbands," Pauline shot back.

Pungu had heard that women procured charms from old Mbanda to use in keeping their husbands or in snatching other women's. It was Bambi who told him this. Old Mbanda used to be the Vultures' juju man before he was replaced after his ability to procure wins for the Vultures died off. He seemed to have restructured his venture by giving illness and causing sickness, preparing poisons and charms. According to Bambi, Maura was one of Mbanda's regular clients, and didn't pay for the services she received. Pungu wasn't sure which report was fake or not. All he heard, and had confirmation about, was that Maura was an expert home-breaker. Pungu had heard his father say so and he had seen Samuel's father pack Samuel's mother's box and throw it out of the house after they quarrelled angrily, with Maura's name coming up repeatedly. Being described in public by the nature of her most prized occupation brought out the tigress in Maura. And the chorus of jeering that ensued fuelled her for an inevitable fight.

"What did you just say?" Maura asked in a menacing hiss.

"You heard me, witch woman, husband snatcher. That is why you can never grow fat." Pauline certainly wanted to say more but she wasn't given the chance to finish. Maura sprang on her with her small agile frame, wound her legs around Pauline's waist, clung and began tearing Pauline's hair, dress, and arms with her fingers.

Pauline staggered backward to keep the clawing fingers from her face. Her foot got caught in a hole and she toppled, and both women fell to the ground. A sudden commotion erupted from the football field as the news of the fight spread like a foul smell blown by the wind. A sea of spectators from the grandstand flowed right across the field to watch the fight on the other side. The referee wasn't given the opportunity to stop the match as the human wave washed by him and the players to gather in a tight circle around the two women rolling on the ground. The crowd cheered and clapped and tapped their feet in amusement while Pauline and Maura tore and slapped and punched at each other.

"Give way, give way," the linesman shouted and pushed his way through the circle of onlookers. He gripped

Maura's slim waist and pulled her off Pauline, whose face and dress were smeared with blood. Maura kicked and slapped about as the linesman carried her like a bag of feathers and marched off towards the main road. Pauline slowly got up with the assistance of a few helping arms.

"Ashiya," some women said in mock pity. Someone offered a wrapper to cover a curious breast that had popped out of a long tear in front of Pauline's blouse. A small crowd ushered her towards the road.

A short while after, the game of football resumed and shortly after the spectators had resettled to watch the match, Pungu's friends, Saul, Sai and Bambi came running towards him, waving their hands and singing, "Black Stars, the only one, Black Stars forever!" When the boys got to where Pungu was standing, Bambi waved him to join them, and off they went running around the field, singing at the top of their voices and waving their hands and flags.

Running around barefooted gave Pungu Alphonse a feeling of freedom. He felt light and loved the feel of the earth on the soles of his feet, especially the warm pebbles heated by the sun. He also liked the cold oily feel of mud as he played under the rain. As for the heated earth, his father said that the heat killed germs that stuck on young children's feet. According to Dikalo, children who imprisoned their feet in shoes both night and day stood a greater risk of not walking properly when they grew up because their toes would surely be destroyed by shoe-germs. As for the usefulness of mud on bare feet, he said mud had extraordinary curative powers. Mud cured water-rain which the dictionaries referred to as athlete's foot. But Pungu had

instead heard the opposite—mud caused water-rain. He
knew his father said this to justify his inability to buy him
shoes. But all that didn't matter now as he jumped around
with his friends waving and hailing the Black Stars of
Bonabato to victory.

B

Pungu's beautiful escape was interrupted by tyres
screeching against the gravelled road. For a moment, he was
confused, disoriented. He wondered how far and how long
he had been gone into the past. It took a couple of seconds
for his mind to bring him back to present reality. And
during this moment, he heard the noise of crunching boots
around the house. He looked up and saw a head wearing a
helmet looking in from the window, a rifle pointing down
at him on the bed. Pungu knew his end had caught up with
him, like the numerous men, women and children killed in
this faceless battle. Fright shut down his mind as soon as he
was dragged out of the room. All the way to the military
jeep, the two soldiers fired questions in French. Pungu
couldn't find the voice to respond: firstly, his mouth
refused to open, and secondly, he didn't understand
French. They tossed him into the jeep which was loaded
with eight armed soldiers.

Slowly Pungu began to come around. The youngest
soldier sitting opposite him determined somehow that
Pungu didn't understand French.

"What you do for that house alone?" the young soldier
asked. "Where the others?" He didn't shout as his
colleagues had done.

"Are you mumu?" another soldier shouted.

An idea jumped into Pungu mind. Given that he hadn't uttered a word since he was caught, he could as well pretend to be deaf. And why should he stop at deaf if he could add dumb?

"Where the others?" the youngest soldier asked again.

Pungu made awkward signs with his fingers and arms before pointing to the general direction of the forest. The men communicated rapidly in French. Pungu did not understand what was said but noticed that the jeep was immediately started and headed towards the road Pungu had used to get home.

"You will take us to their camp now!" one of the soldiers said to Pungu in no kind tone. And to emphasize the seriousness of his words, he nudged Pungu's nape with the cold muzzle of his gun. Pungu nodded to show that he had understood and hoped the man would remove the gun from his neck, but the chilly metal remained pressed against his skin and neck bones. Throughout the drive, the soldiers spoke in French, strategizing on how to attack the tent and kill everyone.

"Let me know when we near," the young soldier said and made signs with his hands to Pungu.

As they drove, Pungu pondered on how they found him. The soldiers must have been doing a routine patrol and noticed that all the doors and windows of most houses were locked since the village was deserted. Opening his window that morning must have drawn their suspicion that someone was hiding behind it.

Pungu signalled to the young soldier as the road narrowed to a grassy footpath. The driver stopped the vehicle and six soldiers jumped down, one of them whisking Pungu down with him.

"Ssshhhh! No noise. You understand?"

Pungu nodded as he led the way through the cocoa farm. Tears of guilt rushed into his eyes as they approached the tent. He had run away only to bring back death with him. The children were standing in a circle around the women under the kitchen-tree, sobbing. As he got closer, oblivious of the soldiers, he realized that the women were using machetes and hoes to dig a grave. They were humming a tune as they dug, with faces wet with sweat, tears and mucous running down nostrils.

Pungu felt a sharp pain of loss in his chest. Maura had died. Big Mama Nyame, hoeing out earth from inside the grave, was the first to see Pungu and the soldiers as she stood upright to rest her waist. She stood still and slowly the others followed her gaze and saw the danger that Pungu had brought home to them. But no one spoke or tried to escape. As though in total submission to fate, the women and children stood and gazed with glazed eyes.

In less than a minute the soldiers had combed the entire surroundings.

"Where the die body?" one of the soldiers demanded. But this time he didn't point his gun at anyone. It hung loose at his side.

Mama Nyame was helped out of the knee-deep hole. She led the way into the tent to where Maura lay wrapped in an old worn bedsheet stained with blood. The young soldier knelt beside the human bundle, pulled the sheet from Maura's face, and suddenly retracted for a second in shock and then bent forward again and began working his fingers around Maura's neck. Pungu noticed Maura's stomach had gone down. But where was the baby?

All of a sudden, the young soldier shot back to his feet shouting some quick words in French.

Pungu watched in fascination as three of the soldiers joined the young one, went on their knees, and after whispering for a moment, picked up Maura's body and carried her out.

"They say she is still alive," Auntie Pauline, who understood some French, said in a voice that quivered with cry and laughter of joy. Another soldier pointed to Auntie Pauline to follow them as he too sprinted behind his colleagues, tracing their way back to where their jeep was parked.

Pungu dropped down on the mat, stretched out his legs, buried his face in his hands and began to cry.

"Where is my pikin?" Pungu heard a voice ask. He raised his head to see who had spoken. It was the young soldier. He was leaning on a wooden pole, eyes almost wet, the muzzle of his rifle buried in the earth. He was asking Big Mama Nyame where his baby was.

About the Authors

Howard Meh-Buh Maximus is a PhD Microbiology student at the University of Buea, Cameroon. His work has been published in *Aerodrome*, *The Africa Report*, *Bakwa Magazine*, *The Kalahari Review*, and *Brittle Paper*. His fiction and nonfiction pieces have been published in anthologies such as *Selves* (An Afro Anthology for Creative Nonfiction), *Love Stories from Africa*, and *Limbe to Lagos: Nonfiction from Cameroon*. He was a participant of the Literary Exchange Program for creative nonfiction between Cameroon and Nigeria, organized by *Bakwa Magazine*, *Saraba Magazine*, Goethe Institute Nigeria and Goethe Institute Cameroon. He is a staff writer for *Bakwa Magazine* and is currently working on the novel that got him on the Miles Morland shortlist 2018.

After his training as an engineer at the National Advanced School of Public Works (NASPW) in Yaounde, **Bengono Essola Edouard** was recruited by the Ministry of Public Works. Prior to that, enamoured with dialogue and aesthetics, he had tried his hand at playwriting and poetry in his third year in secondary school, then at short stories a few years later. He won the 2014 edition of the *Prix de la Nouvelle Séverin Cécile Abéga*, organized in partnership with the French Institute of Cameroon (IFC), with the short story "Le Beau Jardin du Fonctionnaire." In 2017, he won the Bakwa Magazine Short Story Competition with the short story "De Passion et d'Encre." His flash fiction piece, "La Contre-Exposition," won him the first prize in the 2017 edition of the *Cène Littéraire* competition. The same year, he won the National Young Writers' Competition with "Maimouna ou la fatalité."

Dzekashu MacViban is a writer and editor based in Yaoundé. In 2011, he published a collection of poems titled *Scions of the Malcontent* and founded *Bakwa Magazine*. After a one-year gig at the *Ann Arbor Review of Books*, he subsequently wrote for Goethe.de/kamerun, *The Africa Report*, *This Is Africa* and *IDG Connect*. In 2016, he was a writer-in-residence at the Ebedi International Writers Residency. His fiction has appeared in *Wasafiri*, *Kwani?* and *Jungle Jim*. He was runner-up for the *Sonora Review*'s Flash Friday Caption Contest in 2012 and received a Special Mention for the 2016 Short Story Day Africa Prize. He was formerly Editorial Manager at *This Is Africa*. Twitter: @Dmacviban

Wise Nzikie Ngasa was born in Bamenda, North West Region, Cameroon. His short story, "Devils," won third prize at the 2014 Writivism International Short Story Contest in Kampala, Uganda, where he also took part in the Writers' Studio Workshop. His short story, "Clo goes to School," was winner of the 2015 Corruption-free Africa Competition. His stories have also been published in the *Munyori Literary Journal*.

Monique Kwachou is a Cameroonian writer, youth worker and scholar of Gender Studies and Education for Development. She published her first book, a poetry collection entitled *Writing Therapy: A Collection of Poems*, with Langaa RPCIG in 2010. She has since published poems, short stories and articles in various international magazines and anthologies including *To See the Mountain and Other Stories* (2011), *Summoning of the Rain* (2012), *It Wasn't Exactly Love* (2015) and more. She has been national Public Relations Officer for the Anglophone Cameroon Writers Association.

Amadou Bouna Guazong, a scriptwriter, comedian and audiovisual post-producer, holds a Master's Degree in performing arts and cinematography with a specialization in film and TV production obtained at the University of Yaounde I. In 2010, he won the "Grand prix Pabe Mongo" in the *Le camroes* international writing contest. In 2014, he emerged as winner of the *Naples raconte* short story contest organized by the University of Naples in Italy, which published his short story, "Le chacal," in the anthology of the contest in 2015. In 2016, with his short story, "Brrrrrrrrr!", he was a finalist in the Bakwa Magazine Short Story Competition, which was open to Cameroonian writers all over the world. In 2018, he was a finalist in the *Prix des inédits d'Afrique et outre-mer* playwriting contest with his play, *En route....*

Nkiacha Atemnkeng is a Cameroonian writer who works at the Douala International Airport. His works have been published in the Caine Prize's *Lusaka Punk and Other Stories* anthology, *The Africa Report*, *Culture Trip*, *This Is Africa*, *Bakwa*, *Saraba* and *Gyara* Magazines. He attended the 2015 Caine Prize workshop in Ghana, the 2017

Nigeria-Cameroon Literary Exchange Project, and the 2018 Miles Morland workshop in Uganda, facilitated by Giles Foden. He is a Sylt Foundation writing residency prize winner and a Kundslerdorf Schopingen residency fellow.

Momo Bertrand is an award-winning digital marketer and storyteller. Before his 21st birthday, he had launched an African social network, a charity club, as well as a digital agency, www.MomoB.biz. His passion? Using stories as vehicles for change in schools, organizations and communities.

Rita Bakop is a young Cameroonian who lives in Yaounde. A translator by training, she freelances for individuals, corporations and translation agencies. While in secondary school, she wrote a few sketches for the school's theatre troupe, of which she was a member. She would later get into poetry, then short stories. She is passionate about African literature, music, cuisine and sports.

Dipita Kwa was born in Tiko, the South West Region of Cameroon. His publications include: *Times and Seasons,* a novel published by Cook Communications in 2008, a revised and extended edition of which was published by Miraclaire Publishing in 2013 under the title *From the Shadows of Yesterday; Pieces of Silver* (novel), published with Langaa C.I.G in 2010; and short stories in online magazines (*Authorme, Kenagain,* the British Council's *Crossing Borders Magazine*) and in anthologies (*African*

Roar, 2013; New Internationalist's *One World*, 2009; Africa World Press Inc's *Speaking for the Generations*, 2010; Magellan & Cie's *Nouvelles du Cameroun*, 2011).

About the Translators

Hannah Jakobsen is the Editorial Director of Phoneme Media, a non-profit publisher of books in translation. She is also a translator and educator, and is based in Los Angeles, California.

Emma Fredgant is a resident of Portland, Oregon. She received degrees in English Literature and French from Pomona College in 2017, winning the F.S. Jennings Memorial Prize for Excellence in English. Emma returned recently from a yearlong fellowship at New York University Shanghai in China. She looks forward to further pursuing her interests in curation, translation, publishing, and the history of language in the future.

Sign up for our newsletter at www.bakwabooks.com and receive exclusive updates, including extracts, podcasts, event notifications, discounts, competitions and giveaways.

Follow Bakwa Books

Twitter: @BakwaBooks

Instagram: @BakwaBooks

Facebook: @BakwaBooks